About Sally Jenkins and Bedsit Three

Having wowed critics, competition judges and readers alike with her ⟨…⟩ ⟨…⟩ intriguing short stories, it's no surprise th ⟨…⟩ but novel *Bedsit Three* should alread ⟨…⟩ ⟨…⟩nner that's attracting attention.

This tale c ⟨…⟩ ⟨…⟩e won the inaugural WordPlay F ⟨…⟩ an Award and was also shortlisted ⟨…⟩ ⟨…⟩d-Kobo-Berforts Open Day Comp ⟨…⟩ ⟨…⟩riting Magazine/McCrit Competiti⟨…⟩

Michael ⟨…⟩ ⟨…⟩nd Managing Director of WordPlay ⟨…⟩ Bedsit Three, "This novel is well-constructed, w⟨…⟩ ⟨…⟩itten, and well-edited. But it's also far more than that. It's a book that elicits emotional reaction, drawing the reader into the story and placing him or her in the middle of the action page after page. A word of warning to anyone who picks this book up: be prepared for a sleepless night, because you won't want to put it down until you get to the end."

Sally, her long-suffering husband, Paul, and two grown-up daughters, Eleanor and Heather, live in Birmingham with their goldfish, Reg. The wilderness of Sutton Park is close by, a wonderful place for wandering, plotting and creating characters.

By day she is a computer programmer but after hours Sally lets her imagination and pen run riot. When she's not hammering at the keyboard she gets her exercise bell ringing and attends Bodycombat classes.

Find out more about Sally and follow her blog at www.sally-jenkins.com.

BEDSIT THREE

by

Sally Jenkins

Bedsit Three

Prologue - Two Weeks Earlier

Four in the morning and the trench still wasn't finished. It was two feet deep in its mid-section but petered to only six inches at either end. The length and width were enough for his purpose - she was only a slip of a girl - he just needed more depth. But time was running out. Soon the sun would rise and the world would wake up.

He drove the spade into what he thought of as the 'head' end, beneath a scruffy rosebush. It was the best he could do by way of a floral tribute. The plant's leaves would never be properly green again and it still carried the dead heads of summer but he could hardly lay a wreath here.

The pile of earth alongside the trench was growing. What if it wouldn't all fit back inside the hole with the body? There was no time or means for disposing of topsoil.

Sweat was running off him despite the coldness of the night. His gloves were too big and made the spade difficult to handle. It grew heavier and heavier in his tired arms.

He moved round and tried to deepen the foot end of

the grave but the shovel continually hit stones. The noise unnerved him and he was forced to proceed more cautiously, bending to remove stone after stone. When his spine started to complain he gave in. Surely she wouldn't need that much depth.

His plastic digital watch showed another fifteen minutes had passed. He'd started digging half an hour after the last of the lights in the bedsits had gone out. From inside the broken-down shed at the bottom of the garden he'd watched the windows in this house, and those on each side, plunge into darkness one by one. Then he'd managed to keep his cool and wait a little longer in case there were any last minute trips to the toilet or forgotten hot water bottles. Finally he'd started digging with the spade he'd bought that afternoon. He'd watched enough television crime drama to choose somewhere large and busy and pay cash so he wouldn't be remembered.

A light went on in a top floor flat. The curtains were open. He froze and then flung himself headlong into the grave. The lady of the night must have returned from her evening's business.

His warm sweat turned icy as he lay pressed against the damp mud, his head turned to one side so he could breathe. The sound of cars passing the front of the house was becoming more frequent. This was all taking much, much longer than he'd anticipated. He was rigid with tension. If the stupid whore didn't hurry up, it would be time for the rest of the house to start waking. From the corner of his eye he saw her curtains close and then the light went out. At last he could fetch the body.

Struggling to keep his hand steady, he unlocked the front door of the Victorian villa. The dim hallway smelt of stale cooking. A stray autumn leaf crunched between his foot and the grimy tiled floor. The single lightbulb cast shadows on the chipped ceiling rose and gave barely enough illumination to ascend the stairs.

His room was on the first floor and she was all trussed up in a tarpaulin ready to go. The tarpaulin had been a stroke of luck. He'd found a couple of them, along with a rusty camping stove and a rucksack, when he'd first moved in. They'd been stuffed in the back of the wardrobe. He'd kept them 'just in case'.

He hoisted the body on to his shoulder and, opening the door an inch, he double-checked that the stairwell was deserted. Then he walked as quietly as he could down the stairs. She was a dead weight over his shoulder. A couple of times he stumbled but managed to right himself before he and the corpse clattered down the staircase.

There was no back door accessible to the residents so he was forced to go out the front and then negotiate the full-height wooden side-gate and narrow path to get to the garden. He heard her head crack against the building as he squeezed his bulk past an old bike and the garden rubbish wheelie bin that was never used.

Then the grave was in front of him and he tipped her in. She ended up the wrong way around, with her feet by the rosebush. That bothered him but there was no time to mess around. He picked up the spade and started shovelling earth back into the hole around her and on top of her. Every so often he stopped and patted down the soil so he could fit more in.

When he'd finished, all that could be seen was a gently rising mound of freshly dug earth. No one ever came into the garden. No one would ever get suspicious. No one would ever see that the ground had been disturbed. Burying her close to home was a risk but it would have been even riskier to cart her body off somewhere else.

He dumped the spade in the broken-down shed. The gloves meant it was free of prints.

It was time to empty bedsit three and leave.

Chapter One

"Mum! There's a monster! It's under the bed!"

Sandra was startled from her doze in front of the television. She groaned, wrenched herself from the settee and stepped behind the thin chipboard partition that separated seven-year-old Halifax's sleeping area from the rest of the bedsit.

"Mum!"

"I'm here, sweetie." Sandra sat down on her daughter's narrow single bed. "There are no monsters and I'm watching TV just the other side of the partition. There's nothing to make you scared."

"Sleep with me, Mum. Please!"

"There's not enough room for us both in your bed. You've got Bunny, Tigger and Annabelle to cuddle up to."

Sandra arranged the two cuddly toys and the lifelike baby doll alongside Halifax. She hoped her daughter wouldn't insist that the two of them sleep together. It was physically possible for them both to squash under the pink Barbie duvet, but no adult could enjoy quality sleep in such a tiny space. Sandra wouldn't mind a restless night if she could catch up on her rest while Halifax was at school the next day, but her shifts in the supermarket café plus the ironing she took in wouldn't allow that.

She'd tried to get a job waitressing in a proper restaurant where tips would boost her minimum wage income. Nobody tipped the skivvy wiping greasy tables in a supermarket café. But with Halifax she couldn't work evenings and no one wanted her for the lunchtime shift only.

"What if I put my head on your pillow for a little while?" Sandra tried to compromise with her daughter. She knelt down and then leaned over so that their heads nestled together.

"That's nice, Mummy," Halifax whispered.

Sandra stayed perfectly still, trying to ignore the increasing ache in her neck, until she heard Halifax's breathing slow to the gentle rhythm of sleep. Then she crept away and put the kettle on for her bedtime tea.

There was a noise at the door. Sandra stiffened.

Someone was fumbling with a key in the lock.

She glanced across at the partition. Not a sound from Halifax.

She crept to the door and listened. There was someone on the other side. She could hear cursing and then the scratch of metal on metal as whoever it was tried to put a key in the lock again.

"That woman's given me the wrong bloody keys," muttered a man's voice.

"Go away!" Sandra whispered as loud as she dared through the wood. "You've got the wrong flat. You don't live here."

"Yes, I do," said the voice more loudly; a posh southern accent. "I'm the new tenant of this flat. I should be asking what you're doing in there."

Halifax was beginning to whimper in her sleep.

"Go away!" she hissed again, one eye on the

6

chipboard partition.

"Open the door and I'll prove this is my flat!"

Halifax made a mumbling noise. Sandra didn't want her daughter to wake again. She put the safety chain in place and opened the door as far as the metal links would allow. Whoever was on the landing held a smartphone up to the gap between the door and its wooden frame.

She read an email from the landlord of Vesey Villa.

"You've got the wrong flat. This is flat two. You're supposed to be in flat three. It's across the landing," she said, pushing the door closed.

"Sorry, can you repeat that? I can hardly hear you. Or could you open the door again?"

"No, I bloody well won't open the door. You might be a pervert. Try the flat across the landing." She raised her voice for the last sentence.

She'd got an imbecile as her new neighbour, a middle-class poncey southern imbecile by the sound of it. And he must be very down on his luck to be moving into Vesey Villa. He was probably some sort of weirdo misfit.

After the man's footsteps had crossed to the other flat she stuck her head around the partition. The cuddly toys were all over the floor but her daughter was still asleep.

Sandra re-boiled the kettle. As she tried to add two teaspoons of sugar to her mug, the white crystals bounced on to the scratched worktop and she realised her hand was shaking. Had the man been so inclined, he could have thrown his weight against the door chain and forced his way into the flat. She should never have opened the door at all so late at night. Being a single mum was tough in too many ways. It made Sandra want to roll up into a ball like a hedgehog and use her spikes to keep all the bad things away. Her friends with partners didn't realise how lucky they were.

***

The sound of voices leaving the pub woke Ignatius. It must be closing time. His body felt stiff and cold but mostly it felt old. He'd been sleeping in his car for two weeks now and each day he felt worse. The old Volvo was large but not large enough for a man to stretch out in.

He should move on as he'd planned. Get a new job and find somewhere to live. Or at least drive to another part of the country. Sooner or later someone from the Golden Swan would grow suspicious. He'd thought it would be easy to get into the car and leave but Maxine and Mother exerted a strange pull over him. And today he'd realised he couldn't do without his cardboard box of special possessions any longer.

There was no moon tonight so the only illumination came from street lamps. A leaflet had been shoved under the windscreen wiper as he slept. Ignatius got out to retrieve it. The paper was damp and almost tore as he lifted it from the glass.

"Can the dead really live again?" it asked in large gold lettering on a purple background.

Ignatius almost dropped the flyer in fright. It was a message from beyond. He looked around, half expecting Maxine to step out from the shadows followed by Mother.

Trembling, he peeled the sodden, folded paper open. Random phrases jumped from the page:

"God has resurrected humans before. He can do it again."

"There is going to be a resurrection."

8

Ignatius was filled with both hope and fear.

There was a contact number on the back. Ignatius carefully spread the leaflet on the dashboard of the car so it could dry. It might show him how he could see Maxine and Mother again.

Chapter Two

Ian dumped his holdall inside bedsit three. There was a scattering of letters on the floor and he bent to pick them up.

Almost all of them were addressed to I. Smith. One envelope carried the previous tenant's full name: Ignatius Smith. Ignatius seemed an odd name for a bedsit dweller. It conjured up an image of a university professor immersed in Latin and Greek scripts and living in wood-panelled rooms in Oxford or Cambridge, the antithesis of the woman he'd just spoken to across the landing.

Her accent was broad. She'd stayed out of sight behind the door but Ian could imagine her - bleached hair with dark roots like the barmaid who'd given him the keys to Vesey Villa, crêpy skin from too much drink and too many cigarettes, tarty clothes and heavy makeup. The woman in Amsterdam had been attractive in that cheap, blingy sort of way. If he hadn't been drunk he'd never have slept with her.

Ian looked at the letters again. They were all official-looking apart from one hand-written envelope, which bore only the name 'Maxine'. There was no stamp or address. It must have been personally delivered.

The flat smelt of long-ago cooking and reminded Ian of the cheap digs he'd had during his second year at university. The year he'd fallen in love with Josephine.

Josephine had been one of the quiet ones on his Economics course. She'd kept herself to herself and he'd barely registered her existence in his first year of student partying and drinking. She was blonde, slim and very intelligent. Ian discovered she was also witty and could make him laugh with her sharp observations about the world.

"What a lovely girl," his mother had said the first time he'd taken Josephine home. "Make sure you treat her well and hang on to her."

Ian took total responsibility for their divorce. It had been his stupid mistake.

Last year, Josephine had left for a new job in the Midlands, taking Marcus with her. Although they were no longer married Ian had been devastated: he'd lost his son as well as his wife. It was impossible to be a real father when the only times he had with his son were alternate weekends.

On the weekends that Marcus stayed with him, Ian's elderly neighbour, Mrs Drinkwater, used to bring round an array of baked goodies.

"That poor fatherless boy," she would say to Ian. "He needs feeding up with some good home baking."

"He's not fatherless!"

The description had cut Ian to the core. He'd done his damnedest to see Marcus as often as he could. But the long-distance father-son relationship had been a struggle. Ian had worried that Marcus's childhood was going the same way as his own. So in many ways his redundancy had been a relief. It had given him the opportunity to move nearer to his family.

This bedsit was only temporary. In a couple of

months he'd have a job and then he'd rent a proper flat with a spare bedroom for Marcus to stay over, and eventually he'd buy a house. Then he'd let his seven-year-old son choose décor and furniture that would make his room special for him.

Now it was almost midnight, too late to unpack properly and clean the place up. He'd empty the car of all his boxes and bags and then go to bed.

Half an hour later, Ian dug his sheets out of the holdall and went to make up the double bed. He recoiled when he saw the splodged yellowing stains on the mattress. It felt cold and possibly a little damp. He dug a couple of bath towels out of his suitcase and placed them on the mattress as a barrier between him and the grimy upholstery. Then he tucked in the clean sheets and fetched his duvet.

Sleep was a long time coming as he imagined who might have used the bed, and everything else in the room, before him. The landlord had told him there was a daily cleaner to keep things 'shipshape'.

"Maud from the pub does the bathroom, hall and staircase. But the rooms are the tenants' responsibility."

"What about cleaning them between tenants?" Ian had asked, wary of what he might be moving into.

"Maud does what she can in the time she has. But I'm sure you'll soon spruce it up to how you like it. Or maybe you've got a lady friend who'll do it for you?" A sly laugh had accompanied the last words.

It was getting light when Ian woke the next morning. He lifted his arm to see his watch: 7:09 am. His bladder was screaming to be emptied.

Ian groaned and looked for something to throw on for a visit to the bathroom. He didn't possess a dressing-gown and the urgency to pee was too great to spend time getting dressed properly. He pulled yesterday's jeans over his boxers and grabbed a jacket. Then he walked barefoot on to the landing.

The communal bathroom had seemed clean but tatty when he'd paid a quick visit the previous evening but in the growing daylight it looked far worse. The toilet pan was stained brown, there was a long black crack in the porcelain sink and the tide-mark around the bath was disgusting. So much for Maud and her cleaning.

Ian washed his hands and splashed cold water on his face. He cursed when he realised he hadn't brought a towel into the bathroom with him. He was forced to drip his way back to the bedsit and was dry before he'd managed to locate a hand towel at the bottom of his suitcase.

With his stomach grumbling for breakfast, Ian rummaged in the box of food he'd thrown into the car. It was months since he'd done proper supermarket shopping. Living from day to day and grabbing meals from the takeaway had become a bad habit. He found half a packet of brown rice, a tin of kidney beans, five assorted packs of Angel Delight (Marcus's favourite when he came on his weekend visits), an out-of-date can of fruit salad in syrup and, his breakfast staple, two boxes of Weetabix. There was no milk, tea or coffee but he did have a tin opener.

He ate the fruit salad with a fork straight from the tin. It didn't seem to have suffered from going six months beyond its best-before date. Then he poured the thick, sweet syrup into a glass and drank it. It left him feeling an odd combination of both hunger and sickness. He needed to buy some proper food.

As he came out on to the landing for a second time, a young purple-haired woman in leggings and Doc Martens emerged from flat two with a little girl in tow. There was an awkward silence as the two adults stared

13

at each other.

"Good morning," Ian said.

The young woman appeared to be in her early twenties and looked as though she belonged in the Big Brother house or an episode of Wife Swap. Her hair was spiky and her nails were a similar lurid shade to her hair and they were much too long. Her big eyes were accentuated by heavy mauve and black makeup. She was wearing a baggy purple jumper that finished just below the bum. This choice of top hid any feminine curves she might have had. Despite the hard look on her face, Ian wanted to reach out and touch her. She looked as though she needed protecting from the big bad world. As though she was trying to be brave.

"All right?" she challenged.

Ian wasn't sure whether this was a Midlands form of greeting, whether she was inquiring about his health, or whether it was a local colloquialism for 'what you staring at?' Her tone of voice suggested the last.

Playing it safe, he just nodded in acknowledgement of her words.

"C'mon, Halifax. You don't want to be late for Breakfast Club." Her voice became protective as she started to guide the child to the stairs. "Have you got your sandwiches and reading book?"

It was the voice he'd conversed with through the door the previous evening. He hadn't expected it to belong to anyone so young. He noticed she didn't have dark roots or crêpy skin.

"I must apologise for disturbing you last night."

"S'alright." She had her back to him now as she went down towards the front door.

"Goodbye then. I'm sure we'll bump into each other again soon."

"Yeah. I suppose."

14

Ian watched her make her way down the road until she disappeared around a corner. Then he found a mini-supermarket and filled one basket with milk, bread, butter, fruit and tea and a second with cleaning products. Later he took the car to an out-of-town shopping centre to order a new mattress. Judging from the state of Vesey Villa, the landlord wouldn't respond quickly to pleas for repairs or renewals.

***

Ignatius knew the girl would be out all day. He'd grown used to her comings and goings over the years they'd lived next door to each other. He couldn't remember her name; Maxine had probably told him once. Generally the girl went out just a few minutes before he'd left for work. He'd hear her on the landing checking the little one had everything she needed for school. "Sandwiches? Drink? Reading book? PE Kit?" She'd say it as if she was reading off a list, but not in a nasty reproachful way as Mother would have done.

"Yes, Mummy," the little girl always said.

Most days the pair came back about half past four. Usually he hadn't been there to hear them, unless he'd thrown a sickie with Maxine and they'd stayed in bed all day. Then he'd hear the little girl dancing up the stairs and prattling about her teacher and what the naughty boys had been doing.

"It isn't right that your learning is spoiled like that," the woman would say in response. "Everyone deserves a chance to better themselves."

But Ignatius had no idea about the new bloke's routine. How long would he be gone? From his car in the Golden Swan's car park, Ignatius had watched him lug two heavy carrier bags back to the bedsits. Then there'd been a few hours of inactivity while the man was obviously inside the flat.

He'd seen Maud come to do the cleaning. She'd only been inside twenty minutes before she left again but she must get paid for one hour minimum. It was easy money. As she passed through the car park back to the pub he'd ducked down and tried to disappear into the car's upholstery.

Keeping watch was boring and cold. Ignatius was tempted to have lunch in the warmth of the pub but his money was dwindling. Soon he'd have to start using Maxine's bank account. He'd been trying to avoid that in case someone was monitoring it.

It was early afternoon when the new man emerged again and got into his car. If he was driving somewhere then it seemed reasonable to assume he'd be gone for at least an hour. That was plenty of time for Ignatius to sneak back into his old flat and recover the cardboard box. It was stupid of him to have left it there. How could he have forgotten something so precious?

He unlocked the front door and stepped into the hall of Vesey Villa. There was the usual mess of junk mail and flyers on the hall table and the dirty, unclaimed overcoat still hung on the single available hook. It had been there ever since Ignatius had moved in five years ago, when Mother passed on.

Mother's best friend, Betty, had helped him get the bedsit. She lived in the bottom flat of Vesey Villa and had mothered him when he'd first moved in, taking him the odd home-cooked meal or cake. Then she'd become ill and had been housebound for the last year. Ignatius didn't have the words to ask what her prognosis was but the district nurse went in every day and a yellow clinical waste bag appeared regularly. He guessed it was serious.

When Betty couldn't get to the shops any more, Ignatius had started doing her shopping. He'd taken it upon himself to keep her stocked up with the basics - bread, milk, margarine - which he'd top up with whatever else he thought she might fancy. It made him feel good to see the look on her face when she handed over the carrier bag and she pulled out her favourite chocolate biscuits or ginger marmalade.

"You're such a good boy, Ignatius," she would say. "I wish my own son was half as good as you."

Then he'd walk up to his flat feeling ten feet tall.

These last couple of weeks, it had been difficult keeping Betty supplied. Money was getting tight and he didn't want to be seen. So he'd been darting in with odd things when he was sure no one else was around. But today he had nothing for her.

He walked quietly past her door and up the single flight of stairs to the first floor, the key poised in his hand. If anyone from the other flats saw him he had an excuse ready.

"I'm just picking up a box I forgot to take when I moved out," he'd say. "I've got permission from the landlord and the new man."

When he'd first realised he'd forgotten the box, he'd panicked. Then he'd told himself he was a grown man and didn't need it anymore. But as time passed his bravado dwindled and he longed for the comfort the contents offered. The box was right at the back of the wardrobe and Ignatius had been in such a rush, with Maxine going so unexpectedly, that it had been overlooked.

He'd wondered about brazenly knocking on the door and asking for his box. But that might arouse suspicion and questions from the new man, especially if he'd already seen what was inside it. Or he might ask

17

Ignatius what he kept inside an old Cheese and Onion Crisp box. Ignatius was getting better at lying, but he still wasn't good.

He felt comforted when he saw his name was still outside bedsit three: 'I. Smith'. It had been against the bell by the front door, too. This made the bedsit still feel like his home, so it seemed acceptable to let himself in.

The key wouldn't go into the lock. He turned it the other way up and tried again. It still wouldn't go in. He pushed harder and then tried it the other way once more and increased the force. Still the key refused to fit. Then he noticed that the metal around the lock looked much shinier than he'd ever seen it.

The flaming lock had been changed! The landlord must have done it after he'd left. Talk about a lack of trust! Did he think Ignatius was some kind of thief?

He kicked the door. He swung his leg back and kicked it harder. It wasn't right that he was barred from his own home. He raised his foot again. This time he'd bash a hole in the door and break in!

"What's going on?"

The new tenant appeared on the landing just as Ignatius's foot made contact with the door for a third time. He'd kicked too hard and a stab of pain shot through his foot and into his lower leg. He hopped around cursing.

"What are you doing to my door?"

The man had a posh voice. He didn't belong in these parts. For a second, Ignatius thought he might be the police. He said the first thing that came into his head.

"Promised a mate I'd feed his goldfish. Key doesn't fit though."

"Which flat does he live in?"

"Number four."

"This is flat three." The new man pointed at the words to the left of the door, above the name 'I. Smith.' "Flat four is on the next floor up."

"Sorry, mate. I must have had one too many when he gave me the key last night." Ignatius gave an artificial laugh and headed for the next flight of stairs, limping slightly from the pain in his foot. As he reached the landing above, he heard the door of Number Three open and then slam shut. The goldfish story had been believed. Ignatius felt proud of his self-control and quick thinking.

He gave it a couple of minutes before creeping back down the stairs and leaving Vesey Villa.

Back in the car he took off his sock and examined the bruise developing on his big toe. He'd probably lose the nail. But the thought of his missing box caused him greater pain. He took a deep breath and re-cloaked himself in bravado.

Then he looked at the mauve leaflet with the gold lettering. It had dried out now but the paper had gone crinkly. The thought of the dead living again both excited and terrified him. Would the living dead be exactly as they were when alive or would they be like horror film zombies?

He hoped Maxine's body would once more be soft, pliable and welcoming, and she'd be keen for his company and understanding of his needs.

But how could she be resurrected from beneath the weight of all that soil? She wasn't strong enough to battle through it herself and he wouldn't know when the time had come for her to return to life. She'd need his help. He had to stay close by.

***

Mrs Fortescue had dropped off two canvas bags of ironing. It was Sandra's half-day at the supermarket café and she wanted to get most of it done before she collected Halifax from the After School Club.

"Good afternoon, Sandra. Two bags this week. I hope you don't mind?"

Mrs Fortescue's voice had been carefully neutral as she looked in disdain at the grubby landing and the shabby interior of Sandra's bedsit. Her well-bred politeness reminded Sandra of the new man in flat three. Mrs Fortescue and he were both from the same world and, despite their careful words, Sandra felt they saw her as scum. Vowing to ensure that Halifax would never have to live like this, Sandra positioned the ironing board in front of the television, plugged in the iron and used the remote to fill the room with an afternoon chat show.

Three women sat on a settee discussing a film star's latest red carpet appearance.

"She's gained weight," commented one of the women. "That dress is pulling too tightly over her hips and stomach. She needs to heed the advice on her own exercise DVD."

Sandra bent over the TV screen to see this terrible fatness that had befallen the actress but all she saw was an impeccably turned-out and very beautiful woman waving at the crowds. Every so often she paused on her stiletto heels and posed for a press photographer.

"I bet no one looks down on her," Sandra said out loud.

She picked a dark red silky blouse from the bag and arranged it on the ironing board. When she'd started her business she'd had a payday loan to buy a top of the range ironing board and iron. Sandra's motto was, 'If a job's worth doing, it's worth doing well'. She'd paid back the loan with her first month's earnings and now everything she got was pure profit - as long as no one whispered to the tax man. Halifax's higher education money was not going to be shared with the British government. Her daughter was going to get a university degree, a decent job and a life in which people didn't look down on her.

Sandra adjusted the iron temperature. Once the blouse was done she placed it carefully on a hanger ready to return to Mrs Fortescue. Mrs Fortescue might not treat Sandra as an equal but she'd never had cause to complain about the quality of her work.

"Now it's time to go over to the kitchen and see our recipe of the day," said the woman in the middle of the settee. As well as anchoring this chat show, she was a hairdresser in one of the soaps. Sandra couldn't remember her real name.

"Today we're making Double Chocolate Gateau with Rich Red Cherry Filling," said a male chef in a set of whites that didn't look as though they'd ever been near a kitchen. "It's a nice but naughty treat to go with your afternoon cuppa, girls!"

The women on the sofa giggled.

The program was two-faced rubbish. One minute the three witches were bitching about an actress putting on weight and the next they were urging their viewers to pig out on fattening cake. Did they have no respect for the millions of lonely women who watched this programme for the illusion of company and a break from their difficult lives?

The tally chart beside Sandra was growing. It held a list of different sorts of garment and Sandra added a tick for each one ironed. This made it easy to work out Mrs Fortescue's bill. A blouse was worth four times as much as a handkerchief, for example.

21

"Now before you all rush into the kitchen to make that delectable gateau," middle-of-the-settee woman was saying, "we have some lottery news for you."

The familiar Saturday night lottery draw presenter walked on to the set .He flashed a wide smile.

"We have an unclaimed jackpot prize. Someone in London is going to be very lucky! Check your pockets, under the mattress and down the back of the settee."

The women on the sofa made an artificial show of feeling under the cushions. As if they'd lose their tickets in a stage-set settee!

"There's almost one million pounds up for grabs."

Sandra bought a ticket every week and checked it each Saturday night on the television while Halifax listed all the things they could buy with the winnings. Sandra despaired at the cumulative waste of money on that lucky dip ticket. But buying a lottery ticket gave her a ray of hope every week. And everyone needed hope, didn't they?

Used wisely, only a small win would turn things around for her and Halifax. Halifax's education was the top priority but sometimes Sandra wondered if she too had the capacity to better herself. When she was at school the clever ones in the class had been ostracised and so she'd stuck with the popular gang and wasted her schooldays. Now, at twenty-three, she had no idea whether she possessed the intellect to get a single GCSE, never mind a higher qualification leading to a proper career.

The three women on the sofa were replaced by Sandra's favourite Australian soap and she fell into a steady ironing and folding rhythm as the sun shone on the actors Down Under. Once she got into the zone, she could iron for England and make herself a better hourly rate than the supermarket café paid her. Plus she didn't end the day smelling of grease.

When it was time to fetch Halifax, both canvas bags had been emptied and a row of creaseless clothing on hangers awaited collection. Sandra stepped outside her door and bumped straight into her new neighbour.

"Soz," she muttered, cursing herself for her clumsiness in the presence of someone more intelligent and wealthier than she would ever be. "I'm in a bit of a hurry to collect my daughter."

"No harm done." His smile was condescending. "It happens to the best of us."

Sandra wondered if he was implying that she wasn't one of 'the best of us'. She curved her lips up at the ends to return his smile anyway.

"I don't know how you manage to bring up your daughter when you're squashed together in one of these rooms," he continued, seeming to want to talk. "There isn't room to swing a cat and it must become harder as she gets older, with more homework, bringing friends back, and both of you wanting a bit of privacy."

"I do know that," Sandra said tersely. "But some of us have known no different and we don't have a choice."

"It does explain why so many youngsters go off the rails though, doesn't it?"

"My daughter is not going off the rails. Just because you've got a posh background it doesn't give you the right to criticise how we have to live." She put her hands on her hips. "I was going to say 'Just because you've got money' - but you obviously haven't otherwise you wouldn't be slumming it here."

He looked taken aback at her onslaught. "I'm sorry. I didn't mean to offend you."

"Don't be so surprised that I can stand up for myself. We single parents soon learn it's us against the world."

"Single parent." He paused as though thinking about the words for the first time. "We've got something in common. My son lives with his mum so I'm a part-time single parent."

The man's polite face momentarily dropped its guard and appeared tender. Sandra stared at him. He wasn't bad-looking, probably in his late thirties; there were a couple of greys in his dark brown hair and the beginnings of creases around his eyes. His jeans fitted snugly around his bum and there was no sign of a beer belly. But his expression changed again just as quickly.

"There was a man trying to get into my bedsit earlier. He said he'd come to the wrong flat but I don't think he had. He was fat, forties and balding. Do you know who he might be?"

The sudden change of subject calmed Sandra's prickliness. She cast her mind back a couple of weeks.

"He sounds like the bloke who used to live there. One day he was there and the next he was gone. He must have done a moonlight flit. His girlfriend was nice. She always had chocolate and a kind word for Halifax."

"Was her name Maxine? There's a hand-delivered envelope with that name in the bedsit."

He was talking properly to her now. She started to feel more helpful.

"Yeah, that was it. By the way, I notice you haven't changed the name tag on your door. People will get confused if you leave it there."

"I know. I haven't got round to it yet."

"Typical male."

"What?"

"Men. Whenever there's a job needs doing, they're just about to get round to it. But mostly they never do."

"Give me a chance! I've been here less than twenty-four hours!"

"O.K., you're forgiven. The man before you, he had a funny name. It sounded a bit too clever to suit him, if you know what I mean. It was Ig something. The girl, Maxine, mentioned it a couple of times but I never used it. I hardly saw him."

"Ignatius. I saw one of his letters. By the way, I'm Ian Wolvestone. What's your name? If we're going to be neighbours we ought to know each other."

Perhaps he still wasn't treating her as an equal, but he'd stopped making her feel like something stuck to his shoe.

"Sandra."

"Pleased to meet you, Sandra."

He held out his hand. She took it, noticing how soft the skin was. These were an office worker's hands - an office worker who owned a dishwasher, or had owned one until he moved to Vesey Villa.

"Nice nails," he said, indicating her fingers.

She could tell it was just politeness. He didn't mean it.

"I've got to fetch my daughter now."

She turned and went down the stairs. Maybe Ian Wolvestone was going to turn out O.K. after all. And he was definitely much easier on the eye than the previous tenant.

She wondered what he did in whatever office he worked. She hoped it wasn't the tax office and wondered whether Mrs Fortescue would think it odd if she asked her not to speak to the neighbours the next time she brought her ironing round.

Chapter Three

Ian sat in the bath just long enough to have a quick all-over wash. There was no shower so sitting in the distasteful tub was the only option. He'd scrubbed at it with bath cleaner before getting in but the accumulated rings of scum remained.

He dried himself standing on the cold vinyl and then quickly pulled on his clothes and socks. Josephine wouldn't cope with a setup like this and, despite what had happened between them, he hoped she'd never have to. It was only marginally better than having an outside toilet.

Ian stood in front of the small mirror above the sink in his room, tucked in his shirt and fastened his belt. He needed to look like a smart, respectable father, not a bedsit dosser. Josephine had invited him for supper. He suspected she'd done it out of duty when he phoned to announce his arrival in Birmingham. But whatever her motive, it meant some precious hours with Marcus. He was looking forward to reading his son a bedtime story. He hadn't done it for so long.

His own father had never read to him. He'd left the family home when Ian was a toddler, moving up to Scotland to live with his 'floozy', as Ian's embittered mother still called her. When Ian reached school age he'd been sent to spend one week every summer with his father. He still remembered that first time when he'd been introduced to Diana.

"Diana is my special friend," his father had said. "While you're staying here, she'll be your mummy."

Ian had been confused, not understanding why he needed a different mummy for that week. Diana hadn't a maternal bone in her body. And because of the physical distance between them, Ian hardly knew his father. Those holiday weeks had been a trial for everyone. They'd been the dark spot in Ian's calendar for eleven years.

When his son was sixteen, Ian's father had stopped the visits although he'd continued his generous financial support until Ian completed his Economics degree. Then his father and Diana had turned up for the graduation, his wedding to Josephine, and finally Marcus's christening. Apart from those landmark events, their communications consisted of empty words in Christmas and birthday cards.

Ian's relationship with Marcus was going to be much, much better than that.

Twenty minutes later Josephine answered his press on the doorbell. For a few seconds they stared at each other without speaking. Her aura of bitterness was still there and if Ian hadn't been paying attention he'd have missed her brief empty smile. She seemed unsure what to do next and brushed invisible fluff from her navy trousers and then pulled the matching jacket straight. He guessed she hadn't yet changed from work. Her hairstyle was new. It was cut in a short bob and there were highlights he'd never seen before. He wondered if they were to hide her first grey hairs. Whatever the reason, the style and colour suited her.

"May I come in?"

Josephine stood to one side as he walked into the hallway.

"Shoes," she ordered and pointed at the floor.

He removed his footwear and put them on the rack by the front door.

"New carpets?" he asked as his feet sunk into the pile.

She nodded. He thought of the crippling maintenance payment she was still trying to exact despite his redundancy.

"It isn't your money," she said, as if reading his mind. "I'm an accountant, remember? I moved here for a better job."

"Where is he?"

Josephine gestured into the dining-room where a fair-haired child sat at the table, bent over an exercise book and a calculator.

"How's my boy?" Ian ruffled his son's hair.

"Daaad…Don't do that."

Marcus wriggled away from the gesture of affection.

"Maths homework? I loved Maths when I was at school. Want any help?"

"I've finished."

The boy pushed his book and equipment into a navy rucksack on the floor beside him.

"I need to set the table for supper," Josephine said, indicating they were in the way.

"Shall we go and kick a ball? Or is there a computer game you'd prefer?"

Ian cringed at the hopeful matiness in his voice. A proper full-time dad would know his child's likes and dislikes. A proper dad wouldn't be trying to make friends with his own son.

"I usually watch TV whilst Mum's cooking."

28

"Fine, I can watch TV. Grange Hill and Blue Peter were my favourites. Are they still going?"

Marcus's eyes rolled slightly heavenward.

"I think times have moved on somewhat," remarked his ex-wife as she walked into the kitchen.

"We could take Buster out if you like."

"Who's Buster?"

"My puppy. He's got a box in the utility room. Mum doesn't want him on the new carpets until she's sure he won't pee on them."

Ian felt a pang of loss. He and Josephine had always planned to get a dog when Marcus was old enough to help look after it. Now that stupid half hour in Amsterdam meant he was missing out on yet another thing.

Marcus led his father through the kitchen where Josephine was busy chopping and frying with the extractor fan going at full pelt.

"We're taking Buster out for a walk, Mum."

"Good idea. Wear him out so that we can eat in peace."

"He whines and scratches at the door when we're eating," Marcus explained. "It's like he knows we're having something nice without him. But it won't be long before Mum trusts him on the carpet."

As soon as Marcus opened the utility door, Buster jumped up at his master and started barking excitedly. He was a young black cocker spaniel with a white flash on his chest. Ian bent to stroke him whilst his son clipped on the lead.

Outside, the dog almost dragged them down the road towards a green open space. It was amazing that his scrawny seven-year-old son wasn't pulled over by the excited canine.

"He knows we're going to play Fetch when we get

there. I've got a ball in my pocket."

"Why didn't Mum keep the old carpets until Buster was fully trained?"

"Mum's got a friend and his dog had puppies just after she'd paid all the money for the carpets. We went to see them and Buster wobbled over to me and licked my hand. So then we had to have him."

"Mum's friend is a man?"

Ian's brain had moved from puppies to the disturbing possibility that his ex-wife was seeing someone else.

"Yes, she works with him. He's called Richard."

"Is Richard Mum's boyfriend?"

"No! He's nearly as old as Granddad."

"That's good."

The dog went tearing across the recreation ground.

"He can smell rabbits. There are lots of them here."

They both focused on the dog. It took concentration to keep him in sight and under some faint semblance of control.

Thirty minutes later a text from Josephine told Ian that supper was almost ready and they should go home.

It was an awkward meal during which Ian realised his son had become a foreign country to him. Odd weekend visits and nightly phone calls, when Marcus was often tired or in the middle of doing something else, couldn't replace being a full-time father. Ian had missed parents' evenings and sports days. He didn't know Marcus's friends and had never helped out at Beavers.

However, out of the dark cloud of his redundancy, Ian was now pulling a silver lining. At first it had seemed like the end of the world when the MD had called a meeting of the workforce and announced there were going to be job cuts. But when the initial shock had receded, Ian had realised this was the impetus he needed to up-sticks, move near his son and become a proper father again.

"So when are you going to come and stay the night with me, Marcus?" He resisted the urge to ruffle his son's hair again. "I can drop you at school the next morning."

Marcus hesitated and looked at his mother.

"You don't live in a very nice place, do you?" he said. "People get mugged and murdered on your doorstep."

"Well, I haven't seen any dead bodies!" Ian forced a laugh. "And the neighbours are fine."

There was no need to mention that he'd only met a prickly single mother with purple hair, and an odd rotund man, possibly the previous tenant, who was trying to break into his flat.

"I don't want him mixing with ne'er-do-wells, Ian. Marcus only gets one chance at growing up and he needs to do it in a nice area surrounded by nice people."

"One night in my bedsit won't send him off the rails."

"And he's got homework from school," Josephine continued. "He has to read aloud every night."

"I can help with that." Ian was not going to let his wife and her grudge against him spoil his new life. "I'm literate."

Ian was remembering how much he'd hated having only his granddad on the touchline when everyone else had their dad. There'd been no one to play-fight with and no one to tease him or take him to football matches. That was not going to happen to Marcus.

"We'll see."

Josephine busied herself serving helpings of fruit salad from a crystal bowl. Ian recognised it as one of their wedding presents.

"No, let's make a date now," Ian pushed. "Give ourselves something to look forward to, eh Marcus?"

The boy shrugged and looked at his mum again.

"I think we should start with a short visit for supper first," Josephine said. "I'll come too, just to make sure that Marcus feels comfortable with the situation."

You mean so that you can check out where I live and then come down on me like a ton of bricks when it doesn't meet your high standards, thought Ian.

"O.K.," he said with a bright smile. "What about tomorrow?"

There was nothing like striking whilst the iron was hot.

***

The late news was on Radio WM when Ignatius returned to his car. He'd nursed a single pint all evening in The Golden Swan and things were becoming a bit awkward in the pub now. Maud had started asking questions.

"I see you moved out of Vesey Villa," she'd said.

What did she know? She was only supposed to clean the communal areas, not nose around private rooms.

"Don said you'd done a flit and asked me to do your room a few days ago. I didn't have time but I did push the post under the door. I should've kept it behind the bar here for you but I thought the new tenant might have an address to forward it to. Where are you living now? Don said you scarpered without proper notice."

"I paid him his due."

The greedy scheming thug had made him pay an extra month's rent because he'd given no notice. Ignatius had only complied because he couldn't risk bailiffs or police sniffing around. That's why he was short of cash. It was lucky that he knew Maxine's PIN. Soon he might have to use it, especially since Betty was still dependent on him for provisions. She'd no idea he'd packed in his job and left the bedsit. He made sure he still took her bread and milk every two to three days so she didn't starve.

"So where'd you go?"

"I've got somewhere not far away. It's small but O.K. for one."

"Your girlfriend's gone then?"

Shit. He'd forgotten Maud had met Maxine.

"It didn't work out. You know how it is. She went her way and I went mine." Ignatius thought he should win an Oscar for his improving acting ability. Luckily Maxine and Maud had never hit it off, so Maud would take his explanation at face value.

Maxine hadn't liked going to the Golden Swan. She didn't think it was exciting enough for a night out. Ignatius hated going out. He preferred to stay in or have a pint in a familiar place where he was known. It was just one of the many differences that had appeared between them lately.

"Everyone goes out on a Saturday and I don't mean to that boring Golden Swan. I want us to go out somewhere proper with my mates," she'd whine. "Somewhere we can dress up."

On these occasions Ignatius had to go with her. He couldn't let her go on her own. She might not come back or she might start seeing someone else. Maxine belonged to him. She was the first girlfriend he'd ever had and she was going nowhere without him.

But in the end she did do something without him. She sneaked off and destroyed something precious to him. She'd told him about it later and she'd even seemed happy about what she'd done. But he hadn't let her get away with it. Oh no. He'd paid her back: an eye for an eye and a tooth for a tooth.

She'd imposed her will on him just as his mother used to. Like two peas in a pod they were, and they'd both got what they deserved. Well, he hoped they were happy together - burning in hell!

The thought gave him a moment of superior satisfaction before the black well of emptiness opened inside him again. He needed them back to fill the void. He wanted someone there to tuck him in at night and kiss him. He wanted someone to make mashed potato and custard. He was lonely. He fingered the resurrection leaflet in his pocket. Perhaps now they'd been taught a lesson they could come back and do things his way.

All he had left of Mother and Maxine was in the cardboard crisp box in the bedsit. That box also held the only souvenir of his son. The boy who never was. The thought of him gave Ignatius a lump in his throat and he had to blink hard. Without Mother, Maxine or his son, the only thing that could offer Ignatius comfort was Teddy Bear. But he was in the cardboard box, too.

Perhaps he should be brazen and just ask to be let into the flat because he'd accidentally left some things behind. But he couldn't do that now because of the stupid lie he'd told about feeding goldfish.

His only option was to break in.

Chapter Four

Sandra could see Ian's bum sticking out of the under-stairs cupboard as she went towards the front door with Halifax. It looked firm and muscular beneath the taut denim. If they knew each other better she'd have given it a gentle slap.

"Hiya!" she called, feeling neighbourly.

His legs staggered backwards out of the cupboard and the upper part of his body sprang from horizontal to vertical. His head banged against the doorframe and he cursed.

"Soz. I didn't mean to make you jump."

"Good morning." Ian turned towards her, rubbing his head. Then he gestured towards Halifax. "Sorry about my language just then."

"No worries. She probably hears worse in the playground every day." Sandra looked at her watch. "And that's where we're off now. What are you looking for in that cupboard?"

"The Hoover. But the flex is all tangled around something else."

"The carer for the woman in Flat 1 gets thirty minutes per visit and never has time to put it away properly. Let me help."

Sandra knelt down in the cupboard doorway. She felt Ian lower himself down next to her. They were almost, but not quite, touching. The one centimetre gap between them prickled with tension. Sandra wondered what would happen if the gap closed and their thighs met. Was Ian feeling this electricity too, or would it just turn out to be a terribly embarrassing moment? She leaned further into the cupboard, tracing the path of the flex with her hand and trying to hold her body away from Ian. She disentangled the flex from a dustpan and an old mop.

"Done it!"

Ian backed away as she manhandled the reluctant vacuum cleaner from the cupboard.

"Thank you."

His smile reached all the way to his eyes. Sandra felt her stomach do a little somersault.

"Mummy!" Halifax tugged at Sandra's hand. "We have to go to school."

Sandra turned away from Ian and followed her daughter out of the front door. She felt weird, as though someone had just cast a spell on her. Falling for a man would do her no good at all, even if he did smile with his eyes. Every man let you down sooner or later and Sandra wasn't going to wait around for that to happen. She was on a mission to build a better life for herself and Halifax.

The hurdle was her lack of qualifications. She'd picked up the adult education brochure from the local college at the beginning of September and worked out what courses would be most useful: English, Maths and IT. One extra shift a fortnight at the supermarket would cover the fees but she hadn't enrolled. She was scared the other students would be more intelligent than her. She was scared she wouldn't be able to keep up with the class and the money would be wasted. But she was even more scared of doing nothing and watching Halifax's life take the same path as her own.

***

Ian analysed his under-stairs encounter with Sandra. It had required self-control to maintain the gap between their bodies; he'd been strongly tempted to let his thigh brush hers. But even with no actual touching there had been electricity. It was a feeling he remembered from the first few times he'd sat next to Josephine in a lecture before they'd started going out. But Sandra wasn't another Josephine. The only things the two women had in common were their independent spirits and luscious figures. Sandra must be around fifteen years younger than Ian and their backgrounds couldn't be more different. Getting involved wouldn't be a good idea, no matter how attractive they found each other. He had to focus on his reasons for moving to the Midlands: to spend time with Marcus and, possibly in the very long term, to persuade Josephine he was once again trustworthy.

The Hoover sounded like a faulty jet engine when Ian switched it on and he feared it might explode or self-combust. But once it was up to full volume it did the job against the accumulated dirt inside the bedsit's front door and ate up the crumbs alongside the bed and the settee.

Ian wiped the skirting boards and picture rail with a damp cloth and grimaced at the amount of black dust it collected. Then he scrubbed at the mini-cooker in the corner of his room and gave the windows a wash too. There was nothing he could do about the outer side of the panes; without a ladder, the grime would have to remain.

Next was the decision about what to feed Josephine and Marcus. Josephine was big on green vegetables and everything being home-made. Last night they'd had chilli con carne made from scratch, and Ian knew it would have included carrots, courgettes and peppers, all carefully grated to an unidentifiable size so they didn't incur the wrath of Marcus.

Marcus would want junk. Chips would be high on his list along with a burger or sausages and baked beans. He'd have to tread a thin line to please both of them, but he needed to do it if his son's visits were to become a regular, pleasurable activity for all.

Ian glanced at his watch. The new mattress was due to be delivered before 1 p.m. 'Sweet Dreamz' had refused to give him a more exact time. He drummed his fingers on the freshly disinfected table, waiting to be allowed to go out shopping. Just before 1 p.m. the doorbell went. He galloped down the stairs.

There was one man on the forecourt manoeuvring a polythene-wrapped double mattress out of a 'Sweet Dreamz'-emblazoned van. There was no sign of a driver's mate.

"Do you want a hand?" Ian looked up at the leaden sky, which was already releasing the occasional large wet droplet.

"Shouldn't do. Insurance, you know? But really it's a two-man job. Wayne didn't turn up this morning - his wife's gone into labour. Premature. Reckon I'll be on my own for the next couple of days at least."

The drops were becoming frequent now. Ian lifted one end of the new mattress and tried to hurry the man indoors. Inside the flat they leaned the mattress against the wall. The man pointed at the bed.

"You want that old one taking away?"

Ian nodded. Together they carried it out to the van.

"Have a good day."

Ian raised his hand to wave. But the man showed no sign of climbing into the driver's seat. Belatedly, Ian realised he was waiting for a tip, even though Ian had done half the work. He handed over a two pound coin. The action brought Amsterdam back into his mind. The girl had demanded the money up front, and when it was over there'd been an uncomfortable few minutes during which guilt and shame had overwhelmed Ian. In a futile effort to cleanse himself he'd pushed another twenty Euros into her hand before she left his hotel room.

"Thanks a lot, mate."

The driver hopped into his van, wound down his window and gave a thumbs-up sign. Ian returned the gesture awkwardly.

On his way to the mini-supermarket, he dropped the bedding and towels that had covered the old mattress into a launderette offering service washes. He requested the hottest boil wash possible. Later, he retrieved clean sheets from the suitcase he'd stuffed into the bottom of the wardrobe.

As he was pushing the case back into place, it hit an obstacle and would go no further. Ian ferreted around in the darkness and retrieved a large cardboard box. 'Fletcher's Cheese and Onion Crisps' was printed in big letters on all the outside faces. It wasn't Ian's box.

The flaps were folded closed and there was nothing to indicate who it might belong to or what it might contain, assuming that the original crisps were long gone. It didn't feel heavy. Obviously the previous tenant had decided to abandon his rubbish rather than take it with him.

Ian unfolded the cardboard flaps. The first thing he

saw was the bear. Around twelve inches high, it was old and well-loved with worn brown fur. Ian picked it up and examined it. The Antiques Roadshow had taught him to look for the Steiff label in the animal's ear. But there was nothing to indicate it was anything more than a child's well-loved toy. He put the teddy into a sitting position on the floor and leaned it against the wardrobe.

Then he delved into the box as if it was a lucky dip. He pulled out a small, shiny, cardboard box decorated with purple pansies. A sticker on the front told him it contained ten notelets plus envelopes, suitable for all occasions. The cards had to be a female possession; no self-respecting man would send a thank-you note written on such floral items. Did this mean a couple had lived in the flat before him, not just Ignatius on his own? He remembered the envelope hand-addressed to Maxine and Sandra's mention of a girlfriend.

Ian peeked inside the small box: six notelets remained. He placed them next to the teddy and put his hand in the crisp box again. He was beginning to enjoy himself. Nosing into someone else's life was fun.

This time he found a scrap book. Ian recognised it as the sort he'd bought from W.H. Smith for Marcus when he was younger. Marcus had daubed paint on the pages and then glued shiny sweet wrappers and autumn leaves on top to make a collage. It was immediately after the Amsterdam incident. Josephine was walking around like a bear with a sore head and the least little thing caused her to blow her top. She'd gone off at the deep end when she found the pair of them working on the dining room table with the messiest materials possible.

This scrapbook was only half full and all it contained were newspaper cuttings.

"Multi-Storey Death - Open Verdict"

"Woman Found Dead at Foot of Multi-Storey Car Park"

"No Suicide Note - Open Verdict"

Ian scanned the headlines. They all seemed to relate to a Winifred Smith who had either fallen or jumped. There had been no witnesses and no suicide note. According to the reports, none of her friends had thought she was suicidal. Only her son, Ignatius, had said she might have jumped.

Ian paused with shock when he read the son's name. The cuttings related to the death of the previous tenant's mother.

"Mum never got over Dad's death," Ignatius had said in court. "I did my best but when I was out at work she was so lonely. I'm not surprised by what happened."

The report said the son had broken down in court and wept for his mother.

"I should've done more," he sobbed, "but I had to earn a living."

The cuttings were dated five years earlier.

Ian closed the scrapbook, feeling awkward at having invaded a stranger's grief. But the cuttings had caught Ian's imagination and now he had to keep nosing until the crisp box was empty.

Next out was a dog-eared address book. There was a photo of a cute tabby kitten on the front wearing a collar made of daisies. The writing inside was rounded and childish. The picture of the cat plus the knowledge that few young males bother to record the addresses of their mates made him suppose the address book had also belonged to someone who'd shared the flat with Ignatius.

He reached into the box once more. At first he thought it was empty, but when he investigated the corners he found a couple of photos and a white plastic stick. Both pictures had rough vertical tears, about an inch long, in their top edges. As though someone had been about to tear them in half and then stopped.

One photo showed a woman in a restaurant. She had a half full glass of wine in front of her and was laughing at whoever was behind the camera. It was a perfectly normal picture except for the giant 'X' scrawled across her face in red marker pen. It was as though the person wielding the felt-tip had wanted to obliterate her.

The second picture showed the same woman sitting in one of the armchairs in the bedsit. The grubby floral pattern of the upholstery was plainly visible. Again she was grinning for the photographer; again, red ink stained her face.

There must have been a very un-amicable breakup. Maybe she'd had an affair. Ian wondered why Ignatius hadn't destroyed the pictures completely if he hated the girl so much.

When he examined the white plastic stick more carefully he realised it was a pregnancy test, similar to the one Josephine had used years ago. She'd missed a period and they'd both been so excited by the possibility of a brand new life. Holding hands tightly, they'd watched the result appear on the stick together. Josephine had the fingers of her free hand crossed, desperate for the result she wanted.

Her squeal of joy had almost deafened him. He'd lifted her off her feet in a great big hug and suggested opening the bottle of bubbly left over from New Year.

"I don't think so," Josephine had said, patting her flat stomach. "No more alcohol for the next nine months. This baby is going to have the most perfect start in life."

And Marcus did have a perfect start in life - until he was a toddler and things went sour between Ian and

Josephine.

Looking down at the pregnancy test in his hand now, Ian couldn't remember what the blue markings meant. He didn't know whether this was a positive or negative result. He guessed it must be positive. A couple would be more likely to keep their baby's very first sign of life than a stick indicating there would be no baby.

The box was empty now. It had yielded an odd collection of items but they'd obviously been of value to Ignatius Smith. Ian put them back into the box and folded the flaps shut, making a mental note to put the whole thing out with the rubbish when the bin men were due.

The doorbell went. Grabbing his keys he went downstairs to admit his ex-wife and son.

"This is hardly a suitable place for a youngster," Josephine said as soon as he opened the door.

She held Marcus close to her as she surveyed the Vesey Villa entrance hall.

"It's a bit down at heel," Ian admitted. "But it's hardly a dangerous vice den."

"And you'd know all about those, wouldn't you?"

He didn't rise to the bait.

"It's a bit scruffy," said Marcus.

Ian hadn't taken much notice of the lobby, but now he saw the dingy wallpaper peeling where the wall met the ceiling. A collection of autumn leaves had been blown in by the wind, the edge of the skirting board was badly chipped, and a dirty, unloved overcoat hung by itself on a lone hook. Compare and contrast with Josephine's newly-carpeted and freshly-painted hallway and then discuss. It didn't take a genius to conclude which was the better environment for a seven-year-old boy.

"Let's go upstairs. It's cosier in my room."

43

He automatically put his hand on the small of Josephine's back to guide her. She took a couple of quick little steps forward to escape his touch. Ever since she'd found out about Amsterdam she'd made him feel like something the cat had dragged in. Admittedly, the way she found out wasn't good.

Josephine had borrowed his laptop to post a photo of Marcus on Facebook. She'd been dropped into his account because he'd checked the 'keep me logged in' box. And there, staring her in the face, had been the post from Stu at work. He'd put up a drunken photo of them all outside a bar in Amsterdam and added the words, 'Conference finished. Now we're nicely oiled and ready to try the Dutch ladies of the night'.

Initially Ian had tried to deny that he went through with the ladies of the night plan, but his honest streak was too dominant and the truth came out. He and Josephine had had a blazing row. Separation and divorce had followed shortly afterwards.

"Do you sleep in here, Dad?" Marcus plonked himself down on the newly-made bed. "And cook? As well as watch TV and stuff?"

"Yep. That's what a bedsit is. It's short for a bed-sitting room."

"What about the toilet? And the bathroom?"

Marcus was looking around as if he expected to see the doorway to a shiny en suite.

"It's on the landing. I share it with the other residents."

Distaste was written all over Josephine's face. She was still standing by the door, as if sitting down might contaminate her with deadly bacteria.

"You know this is only temporary, until I get a job." Ian didn't want her to think the bedsit was now the limit of his aspirations. "And in a city like this, it shouldn't take long."

"I know but I still don't like it."

Ian ignored the comment. He knew where she was coming from and another row wouldn't help his effort to build bridges. There was nothing he could do to make his current living situation look better.

"Help me make the supper, Marcus. We're having toad in the hole!"

"Yey!" the boy exclaimed and stood up. "Have you got ketchup and chips?"

"Ketchup, yes. Chips, no. But we are going to have jacket potatoes and lots of gravy." Then Ian lowered his voice as he passed Josephine to get the milk and eggs from the fridge. "Low fat sausages and I've got peas and carrots too."

Her facial expression didn't change but she moved to peer over his shoulder as if she was inspecting the interior of the fridge for germs and furry green mould. He stood to one side to give her a better view.

There was no bowl to mix the batter so Ian produced the jam pan Josephine had bought shortly after Marcus's birth. She'd been going through an 'earth mother' phase. That year they'd had jars and jars of not-quite-set strawberry jam. Most of it was still in the cupboard twelve months later, quietly going mouldy. The pan was never used again and it was one of the few kitchen utensils Josephine didn't take with her after the divorce. It had travelled up to Birmingham with Ian, stuffed with CDs, books and other paraphernalia.

Once the toad in the hole was in the oven Marcus lost interest in the cooking. He stared out of the window at the back garden whilst Ian prepared the vegetables.

"Don't overcook them," instructed Josephine. "It kills all the nutrients. You ought to have a steamer. It's the best way of doing them."

First things first, thought Ian, I don't even have a mixing bowl yet.

"We could play football out there," said Marcus.

"Sure."

Ian was chuffed at Marcus' enthusiasm.

"Not today, it's drizzling and muddy," Josephine pronounced, without looking through the glass. "And you're not dressed for it."

Josephine was always antagonistic these days. He wondered if he'd be the same had he found out she'd paid someone for sex. Gaining her forgiveness was a constant uphill struggle but he wouldn't give up.

"We'll do it next time you come." Ian put down the vegetable knife and walked over to his son. He restrained himself from ruffling the boy's hair. "When you come and stay overnight there are lots of things we can do."

"I could bring Buster. He'd love digging in that big mud heap. Perhaps lots of rabbits have burrows under there. Buster would sniff them out; he's as good as those police sniffer dogs. There's no spare bed. Where will I sleep?"

"You can have my bed and I'll go on the settee. Or perhaps I'll buy a folding camp bed. That would be fun!"

"I think the vegetables must be done by now," said Josephine curtly.

Ian wished she'd soften her attitude towards him when Marcus was around. He set the small, scratched dining table with knives and forks and poured orange juice into three glasses. When they'd all sat down he raised his tumbler. "Here's to the three of us and especially to football superstar Marcus."

Josephine was the last to raise her glass. Once they'd

eaten the Greek yoghurt and honey dessert she started making noises about leaving.

"Can we stay a bit longer?" Marcus pleaded. "I brought my Racing Car Top Trumps game. I want to play it with Dad."

It was bad form, but Ian couldn't resist a superior grin at his wife. She put on her 'not happy about this but resigned to it' look and moved from the dining table to the armchair. She inspected the upholstery and used her hand to sweep it clear of imaginary detritus. Finally she felt it all over before sitting down.

The photo of the girl in the armchair with the big red cross on her face sprang into Ian's mind. It must have been taken from the spot where he was standing now. Sunlight featured in the picture, so it had probably been taken during the summer, perhaps only a few weeks ago. The girl had looked happy. What had gone so drastically wrong between the couple so quickly?

Ian could imagine Josephine's reaction if he tried to take her photo now. There would be no smile. But the girl was younger and had probably been posing for someone she loved.

After Marcus had had enough of Top Trumps they drank tea and, when Marcus went to the bathroom, Ian pushed Josephine to specify a date when Marcus could come and stay by himself.

"He's not staying overnight," she said. "It's not proper. He needs his own room. And who knows what might happen in that bathroom. There are a lot of perverts around."

"You've let him go to the toilet by himself now!"

Josephine coloured.

"But what if he creeps out in the middle of the night to go and you don't know? He might be dead by morning, or molested."

They both knew she was putting obstacles in the way for the sake of it.

"Please don't punish Marcus for what I did."

Ian put his hand on Josephine's. For once she didn't pull away, and when Ian looked her in the face he saw a tear escaping from her left eye. Finally she agreed that Marcus could come again for supper, but this time alone.

"Let me come tomorrow, Mum! Please!"

Marcus had walked in on the end of the conversation as he returned from the bathroom. His hands were dripping wet. Quickly, Ian handed him a towel.

"O.K."

Chapter Five

Again, the cold woke Ignatius in the early hours. Even though he'd stretched the sleeves of his fleece over his hands his finger ends were white, and his thin socks and cheap trainers hadn't prevented icy toes. Every limb was stiff.

It was impossible to sleep comfortably in the front passenger seat. Lying down in the back would have been better, but it was piled high with his belongings. For over two weeks now this car park had been his home. Incredibly, he hadn't yet been spotted and asked to move on. He was invisible. Somebody of no consequence in the world. Betty was the only person who'd notice if he disappeared.

His mother had warned him this would happen.

"Ignatius, the world is a huge, competitive place," she'd said many times. "If you are to do well you must work hard and you must stand out from the crowd. Do you understand?"

He would nod and try not to show his terror of growing up and being thrust out into the big bad world without his mother there to tell him what to do. She'd pushed him to excel at everything so he wouldn't become a little man in a big man's world. She made him do rugby and football training, learn the piano and join the Boy Scouts. She'd fought with the teachers to get him into the top stream for every subject and then paid for an array of private tutors so he wouldn't be relegated again. Ignatius's every waking hour was organised to educate him and equip him with life skills so he'd become 'a big man'. There was no time for idleness, no time for messing around with friends.

"When you're rich and successful," his mother said, "there'll be plenty of time for resting or doing whatever takes your fancy."

He'd had no siblings to deflect any of this ambitious mothering, so Ignatius, unaided, had done his best to please her. When his mother thought he'd made the grade, which wasn't often, he was rewarded with a hug and homemade chocolate cake. Those rare moments were as precious as gold.

Sitting alone in the freezing car, Ignatius longed to be close to his mother again, experiencing one of those celebratory moments. He looked at the leaflet about resurrection and wondered. Perhaps her death had been a terrible mistake, but a mistake he might be able to put right. He could start now. He would pay her a visit.

He wriggled across to the driver's seat and turned the key. There was a short pause and then the engine burst into life. It was late and traffic was almost non-existent. After a few miles, Ignatius turned right off the main road without bothering to signal.

And then he jumped on the brakes. He'd almost smashed into the great iron gates of the crematorium.

He sat and trembled. The car had stalled on the tiny stretch of tarmac in front of the gates. He'd hardly noticed the metal monsters before, let alone seen them closed. But someone was watching over him: if he'd had more to drink tonight, he might not have reacted in time. It must be Mother. During daylight hours, he'd often visited the little plaque inscribed to the memories of both his parents, and the gates had never been closed.

Ignatius' father had died twenty-five years earlier and hadn't left them well-provided for.

"I thought we owned this house." His mother had wept with incomprehension at the change wrought by widowhood. "Geoffrey told me it was in both our names."

"Both your names are on the rent book," the landlord had explained. "But if you can't pay the rent, you'll have to leave."

Geoffrey had had no life insurance and little in the way of savings. So sixteen-year-old Ignatius and his mother had thrown themselves on the mercy of the council housing department and the benefits system. For a few weeks his mother was a broken woman and Ignatius had had a respite from the incessant round of out-of-school activities. With no regular wage coming in, such extras were unaffordable.

Then Ignatius's mother had pulled herself together and, despite feeling they were beneath her, she'd taken on three cleaning jobs so she could continue to groom Ignatius into a better man than his father had been. She barely had time to sleep.

"Once you're qualified as a doctor it will be your turn to take care of me," she often said as she flopped into a chair, exhausted.

The maternal pressure on him to reach medical school became too much. Six weeks before his A' levels, Ignatius had suffered a breakdown. He hadn't taken his exams. His mental health had never fully recovered.

He got out of the car. The crematorium gates were

51

padlocked and chained. But it had become imperative to see Mother tonight.

He clutched the wet metal and shook hard. The gates swayed slightly under the pressure and the chain clattered against the ornate bars. He examined this monstrous barrier for possible footholds and began to climb. He was three feet off the floor when the toe he'd injured kicking his old bedsit door began to throb. He looked up for the next handhold but the pattern of the bars changed and there was nothing to grab.

The wind was picking up now and, with Ignatius's weight on them, the gates swung inward as far as the padlocked chain would allow. Ignatius clung to the metal and felt like a little boy too high up a climbing frame, out of reach of his mother's help. The gate swung backwards and forwards. It was dark and cold. No one cared.

"Mummy! Please come back!" he sobbed.

A sudden bright light dazzled him. He blinked rapidly, struggling to comprehend. Was it divine intervention? Was it something to do with his mother's resurrection?

On his left-hand side a fox was slinking from the tarmac drive into the undergrowth. Something dead hung from its mouth. The security light on the crematorium lodge remained on after the animal had disappeared.

There was a movement in a window behind the light source.

"Hey! What are you doing? This is private property! If you're not gone by the time I get outside I'm calling the police."

It took a moment for the words to register in Ignatius's brain. Then he loosened his grip and slithered down the gate, curled bits of metal tormenting his hands and feet. There was no time to examine his injuries. The front door was opening. The man was speaking into a mobile phone. Ignatius didn't stop to listen. He fumbled with the car door and fired the ignition. Without pausing to look for traffic he reversed on to the main road.

The terror didn't leave him until he was a couple of miles away. Then he glanced in the rear view mirror. There was no vehicle on his tail. No blue light following him.

He became aware of an uncontrollable thudding in his chest. His father had died of a sudden heart attack. Ignatius forced himself to take deep breaths to quell the panic.

"This is not the worst thing that's happened to you. This is not the worst thing that's happened to you." By repeating the words he could make himself believe them.

He focused on the most terrible thing that had happened to him. Being told of the death of his son. It had been awful but he'd coped with it. Now he could cope with this.

The thudding in his chest diminished. The heart attack wasn't going to happen. But there was no time to relax; the man at the crematorium might have taken his car registration number. Villains in TV car chases made sharp turns down side roads and ducked into multi-storey car parks. The thought of manoeuvring around the concrete levels of a deserted multi-storey sent a burst of adrenalin through Ignatius. He'd done it before. He'd driven in with a passenger and come out without her. He'd been lucky. The CCTV in the concrete building had been faulty so there was no proof he'd ever been there.

He glanced behind again. The road was long, straight

and well-lit. Nothing was following him. No need to panic. He would find another time to visit Mum.

He turned the heater on full blast and slowed down to give the car time to warm thoroughly before he pulled into a lay-by to sleep. It wasn't a good idea to park at the Golden Swan all the time.

***

Sandra liked autumn. She liked the crisp cold days and the bright weak sunlight that could suffuse the most dismal surroundings with hope. The damp and rain weren't so good, but today wasn't wet. Today the weather was hopeful. That was why she'd given in to Halifax's pleas to go to the playground after school.

She ought to be at home finishing the ironing. It was due for collection in the morning. But if she stayed up late tonight it would still get done. Besides, she and Halifax both needed a boost of vitamin D before the winter set in.

"Mum!" Her daughter was waving from the top of the slide steps.

Sandra watched Halifax crouch down and manoeuvre into a sitting position. She waved at her mum again before giving a push with her hands and sliding downwards. Half-way down, she shuddered to a halt. Halifax lifted her arms in a quizzical gesture that said, 'What's happened?'

Sandra got up from her bench and walked over. "It's not slippery enough, love," she explained. "Some kids must have been walking up it in dirty shoes instead of sliding down."

Halifax rolled her eyes skywards.

"Some people!"

Sandra laughed, recognising the words and facial

expression as her own. You had to be so careful around kids; they picked up and copied the least little thing. Standing on tiptoe, she placed a hand on her daughter's back and pushed. She repeated the action several times before Halifax reached the long flat part at the end of the slide.

"When a few more people have been down it will get slippery again," Sandra explained. "Lots of bums will clean off the dirt."

They both looked around the playground as if expecting a hoard of children to appear from the bushes and start queuing to clean the slide. None did. The playground was deserted.

"Or you can keep going up and down it yourself," Sandra suggested.

Halifax headed for the metal steps again. This time she got a bit further before she stuck. Then she wriggled her bottom in an exaggerated fashion.

"Won't take long to get it working again if I do this," she called.

Sandra was about to warn her daughter she was still wearing her grey school trousers, which didn't have the strength of denim and were more expensive to replace. But she kept her mouth shut. She was the one who'd suggested this activity.

She returned to the bench and escaped into a daydream that involved her sailing through a college course, winning a bursary for university, becoming a teacher and moving to a small house where Halifax could have her own bedroom. There was a man involved too. A man who loved and respected her and was proud to treat Halifax as if she were his own daughter.

A squeal from somewhere among the graffitied playground apparatus made her jump. Her eyes searched out her daughter. Halifax was safe, part-way up the slide steps. The noise came from a little boy who was sprinting towards the climbing frame. The man with him looked familiar but at this distance she couldn't place him. For a while he stood with his back to her and watched the boy, who headed fearlessly for the highest spot on the spray-paint-covered structure.

Eventually the man turned away and seemed to be looking for somewhere to sit. As he walked towards the only bench she recognised him: her new, attractive neighbour, Ian.

"Is it all right if I join you?" he indicated the empty portion of the seat.

"Yeah."

It seemed a redundant question. Would anybody say no?

"Do you come here often?"

Sandra felt both flattered and wary.

"If you're trying to chat me up, that's the corniest line in the book."

"No! That's not what I intended," he said. "I meant the question literally: do you visit this playground regularly with your daughter? I'm trying to make conversation."

"Yes," replied Sandra. "I come here often."

"It's not a pleasant environment for children to play in, is it?"

Sandra had never taken much notice of the surroundings. They were always the same - an invisible backdrop to whatever thoughts and daydreams tripped into her head as Halifax played. Now she looked properly. Graffiti covered all the equipment. Some of it was obscene, some of it quite artistic. The single litter bin was overflowing and seagulls scavenged the fast food wrappers and crisp packets around it. Seagulls?

Shouldn't they be by the sea?

"'s O.K.," said Sandra.

She felt him look at her as though she was mad. She said nothing more and stared straight ahead. He was right, this place was a dump, but she had no other choice. And the last thing she wanted was some poofy southerner invading her patch and rubbishing it. She'd have to live here long after he'd gone and she'd rather not have its awfulness rammed down her throat, thank you very much.

"I don't agree. I think children deserve better. They're our future. If we teach them to value and look after their surroundings, places won't get like this."

Despite her intentions, Sandra found herself turning to look at him.

"Discipline begins at home," he continued. "If we all drilled respect into our children then society would be much better for everyone."

"Is that a dig at me? You think I'm a bad mother just because I'm single and haven't got much money?"

"No! Not at all." He shook his head vigorously. "My ex-wife is more or less a single mother since the … since we … divorced. But I do think children should be brought up by two parents wherever possible. Otherwise they miss out on knowing what a proper loving relationship is all about."

"You're getting a bit deep and preachy for someone just making conversation, aren't you? Can't you just mention the weather and then shut up like most people?"

"It's quite nice for the time of year, isn't it?" he said.

"Yeah, it is."

They sat in silence for a few minutes, surveying the duck pond fifty yards away.

Sandra stood up. "Halifax!" she yelled. "It's time we

were going."

"No, Mummy! Please can I have another five minutes? I promise I'll eat all my tea if I can have another five minutes."

"All right, but ONLY five minutes." Sandra sat back down.

"Why did you … choose the name 'Halifax'?" Ian asked, as though wondering how to phrase the question. "It's very … unusual."

Sandra was tempted to tell him to mind his own business. But she was beginning to realise he was harmless, just out of his depth in a culture a million miles from his familiar territory. It reminded her of that TV programme, Wife Swap, where women from completely different backgrounds are forced to exchange lives for a fortnight.

"Her father was a fan of David Beckham. At least that was his story. I think he actually fancied the pants off Victoria. Anyway, he wanted to follow their example and name our baby after the place she was conceived, which was Halifax. We went there in our last year at school. It was a History trip. Something to do with the Industrial Revolution."

Ian looked shocked. She didn't know if it was to do with the origin of the name or the fact that pupils had sex during a school trip.

"We weren't the only ones doing it." Suddenly it seemed important that he didn't think she was a slag who slept around. "I was the only one that got pregnant, though. The teachers didn't seem to care what we did. They just went down the pub and left us to it. It was my first time."

Sandra placed great emphasis on the last sentence.

"I'm not judging you," Ian said. "I was just interested in the name. It's great that it's so unusual. When you're called something boring like Ian you sometimes feel like part of the wallpaper. I guarantee that as Halifax grows up, she'll be noticed."

Now Sandra wondered why she'd told him about the sex bit. She hadn't told anybody about it being on the school trip before, especially not her mother, who'd have gone to see the head teacher and read the riot act, demanding compensation plus funding for an abortion.

If Sandra hadn't left home, Halifax wouldn't be here now. One way or another, her mum would've insisted on killing the unborn child.

"You won't tell anyone, will you? About the school trip, I mean? I don't want Halifax to find out. Mostly I tell people that I read the name in a book somewhere. I shouldn't have let that twat of a boyfriend... but I was young and away from home on a big adventure. Needless to say, like most men, he didn't stay around."

"I won't tell a soul."

For a stupid moment she wanted to throw herself at him and be enveloped in a protective hug. She bet he'd smell nice. He looked like the type who used body spray or aftershave, and not the cheap makes she used to buy for her dad when she was little.

"Five minutes is up," she said, and went to retrieve her daughter from the swings.

The boy on the adjacent swing was working madly, trying to get higher than Halifax.

"This is Marcus," Ian said, coming up behind her. "He's having supper with me tonight and then his mum's picking him up."

"Supper? Isn't that cocoa and a Penguin biscuit? I think you mean tea. If you're going to live around here you'll need to learn the language."

"When in Rome ..." Ian laughed.

They set off back to Vesey Villa together.

59

Chapter Six

Ian felt positive the morning after Marcus's second visit. He stood by the sink in his room, shaving. The tiny mirror in front of him was cracked and discoloured but Ian's life was on the up. It would never be as good as the life they'd had pre-Amsterdam but bridges were being built between him and Josephine and perhaps one day he'd walk across one.

Already he'd achieved some of his objectives in moving to Birmingham. He'd spent two successive evenings in Marcus's company and the boy seemed keen for more. The easy father-son repartee he longed for wasn't there yet but it was early days. There was a lot of catching up to do.

For a second, Ian's mind went back to those painful school holiday weeks he'd spent with his father and 'the woman'. He knew he'd only been invited out of duty, or maybe under pressure from his mother, who wanted to go away with her sister for a break. Whatever the reason, he was forced into the company of virtual strangers all day on long country walks and visits to stately homes. It was obvious they didn't have a clue how to entertain a child. They had even less idea when he became a teenager.

No, his relationship with Marcus was going to be better than that. Much better. Eventually, it might involve Josephine too. For them all to be a family again was what Ian really wanted.

"We went to a terrific playground," Marcus had told his mum when she fetched him the previous evening. "When can I come and see Dad again?"

Ian's heart had swelled with love and pride.

"We'll see," said Josephine.

"Soon? Please?"

"Soon," Josephine had said, not committing herself.

Like a small child counting the number of sleeps until Christmas, Ian pondered his ex-wife's meaning of 'soon' as he finished shaving. A couple of days? A week? Surely not a fortnight?

He reached over and unhooked the mirror from the wall. He intended to replace it with something bigger and better to reflect the way his life was going. His other task today was to buy a copy of the Birmingham Evening Mail; Thursday's paper had the 'Jobs' section. Then he'd dig out his laptop, get connected to Vesey Villa's Wi-Fi and register with as many recruitment agencies as possible. Before long he'd have a salary coming in again.

A bang on the door made him jump. Ian opened the door.

"Can I borrow a cup of sugar, please?"

Sandra was holding out a mug. Ian wanted to laugh. It was a stereotypical neighbour thing but it had never happened to him before.

"Halifax won't eat her Weetabix unless it's sprinkled with sugar and we've run out."

"I haven't got any, sorry."

"Oh!" Sandra looked taken aback. She glanced towards her own bedsit as if not quite sure what to do next. "Maybe she'll eat it spread with jam."

She turned to go, the mug held loosely by her side.

For some reason it mattered to Ian that Sandra understood why he had no sugar. He didn't want her to think he was just being unhelpful.

"I don't take sugar, but I'll get some. One day, someone might visit who likes sugar in his tea. And when I have some you'll be welcome to borrow it."

He was babbling. He should have shut the door after he'd said he didn't have any sugar. What did it matter if Sandra thought he was odd, mean or anything else? He wouldn't be living here long and then he'd never see her again. But the memory of that electric under-stairs encounter was still fresh. Sandra was slim and pretty. He admired her feistiness and suspected her crusty shell hid a vulnerable heart. Maybe they were two of a kind; they'd both loved and lost and were now trying to make the best of things for the sake of their children.

Sandra was moving back towards her own front door, which stood open. Ian could hear the Brummie accent of a local radio presenter.

"Wait! I've got some Sugar Puffs. I bought them in case Marcus stays over. Will Halifax eat those instead of Weetabix? They've got inbuilt sugariness."

Sandra turned towards him. She had 'grateful' written all over her face. She hadn't yet caked on her makeup and her naked look was good.

"Yes, please."

"Come in whilst I find them."

The cereal was in the cupboard under the sink. It was only a small box.

"Take the lot," he said. "I'll buy more when I'm out. And some sugar."

"I'll pay you back," she said. "How much are they? My purse is in the flat."

"No." He couldn't take her money. "It's a gift."

Sandra's face coloured and she scurried away, muttering thanks.

It was too early for the Evening Mail to be in the shops so Ian unearthed his laptop and then checked his phone for the wi-fi network key specified in the landlord's email. Online, he found his inbox full of Amazon deals, restaurant voucher codes and general junk. He was about to start his search for job agencies when he remembered the scrapbook in the box in the wardrobe. The internet might tell him what had happened in the multi-storey car park. He typed 'Death Winifred Smith Birmingham' into Google. It brought up the same newspaper reports he'd seen in the scrapbook. The Evening Mail and the Birmingham Post had both gone to town on the apparent suicide, with pictures of the dead woman as a young bride and then in what looked like a holiday snap taken years later. The Sutton Coldfield Observer, apparently a free weekly newspaper, gave the inquest a full page spread. This cutting wasn't in the scrapbook.

As well as the wedding photo, The Observer carried a picture of Winifred's son. He was standing outside the building where the inquest had been held. Sombrely dressed, he looked careworn and solemn.

"I wish I could have done something to stop her," he was quoted as saying. "But I don't think it was pre-meditated. So what could I have done? It's a guilt I'll live with for ever."

Ian studied the picture again. He recognised the balding head and rotund stomach of the man who'd tried to get into the flat a few days ago, the one who'd said he was feeding his mate's goldfish and had got the wrong flat. Ignatius had been trying to get back into his old bedsit. Why? Ian hadn't noticed anything the previous tenant had left behind - except the cardboard box. But if he'd wanted the cardboard box back, why hadn't he just knocked and asked if he could collect it? Who'd be mean enough to refuse a simple request like that?

Ian remembered the defaced photographs. Visions of blood-stained knives and dead bodies sprang into his head. He shrugged them off. He was being silly. At the back of his mind, Ian still thought of Ignatius as some sort of Classics scholar who'd fallen on hard times; hardly the criminal sort.

There was a knock on the bedsit door.

"Sugar Puffs." Sandra handed him a jumbo size box of breakfast cereal. "I bought them after I'd dropped Halifax at school."

"There was no need ... and this is a much bigger box than I gave you," he protested, trying to push it back at her.

"I'm sure you and Marcus will get through it in no time," she said.

She let her arms hang by her sides so that she couldn't take the box back. Now Ian felt awkward. It was a social situation for which there were no rules. She was giving him more than he'd given her, so now he had to level the playing field by giving her something else.

"Let me make you a cup of tea at least. But I hope you don't take sugar?"

She grinned. "I do but I bought some. Wait two minutes and I'll fetch it."

She returned with a heap of sugar in the bottom of a cereal bowl. As Ian squeezed and removed the teabags from two mugs she stirred the white crystals into one drink and then added milk to both.

"Apologies for the lack of teapot," he said.

"Josephine took it when she left and, being your typical man, I never got around to replacing it. I prefer tea made in a teapot with proper loose leaves instead of a bag. Don't you?"

"Never tried it," she said. "As it comes, brewed in the mug suits me fine, as long as there's sugar. What's this?" Sandra pointed at the scrapbook.

Ian showed it to her and explained where he'd found it.

"I probably shouldn't have snooped. But now I have, I want to know more about what happened to the woman."

Sandra turned the pages.

"Did you know him?" he asked, pointing at a photo of Ignatius.

"He moved in not long after me and Halifax, about five years ago, probably around the date on these cuttings. I didn't see him unless we happened to go out or come home at the same time. I'd never have asked him for sugar."

Ian raised his eyebrows and Sandra coloured.

"He kept himself to himself," she explained. "And he seemed a bit odd." She wrinkled her nose.

Ian showed her the photos of the girl with her face crossed out.

"This one was taken in that armchair, the one over there. Did you know her?"

"She moved in with him about six months ago. I met her on the landing one Sunday morning. She was lugging a suitcase up the stairs. She's a nice girl. Always made a fuss of Halifax if we bumped into each other. There was always a bag of sweets in her pocket, waiting to be shared." Sandra paused to sip her tea, cradling the cup in both hands as though it contained nectar. At the same time she contemplated the two photographs on

65

the table. "She looked a bit pale and peaky just before they left. I thought she might be ill or sickening for something. We used to hear her retching in the bathroom on a morning. A couple of times I had Halifax dancing on one leg desperate to get in there."

"Have you any idea why they left?"

"Nope. But I wish that woman from the top flat had gone instead of them, the one in flat four. It won't be long before Halifax starts asking questions about her."

"What about her?"

"She's a prostitute. I thought you'd have noticed."

For a second Ian wondered if his face made it obvious that he'd once paid for sex and therefore Sandra assumed he was an expert on the vice industry.

"I hadn't. I've seen nothing."

"I think she's been away. She'll be back soon enough. Sometimes she sticks one of her cards against her bell outside the front door. Whenever I see it I pull it off."

"Can't we tell the landlord and get her evicted?"

Josephine wouldn't allow Marcus to stay overnight in the room below a prostitute.

"It didn't work when I asked. But he might listen to you."

***

Ignatius cursed. The warmth of the morning sun on the windscreen had made him sleep late. It was almost noon and he'd missed his chance to drive back to Vesey Villa and watch for the new tenant going out so he could nip in and grab the crisp box.

He'd spent two nights away from the Golden Swan but today he'd planned to return. Betty's milk and bread supplies would be running low and his yearning for Teddy was growing. He'd lain low, choosing a different lay-by each night, in case anyone was looking for him after the crematorium incident.

He stretched as far as the passenger seat allowed and then looked outside for somewhere to relieve himself. A wooden gate in the hedge was slightly open. Ignatius got out of the car and slipped through the gap into the field. There was no one around. He stood against the bush and released his zip.

A dog came through the gate on a taut lead, barking, pulling an elderly lady behind him. Embarrassed, Ignatius tried to turn away from her field of vision. From the corner of his eye he saw her bend and unclip the lead from the dog's collar. The animal shot across the field. The woman stood up and looked around. As Ignatius fumbled to do himself up, their eyes met. She swivelled her head, stared straight forward and stalked across the field after her dog. Her determined walk and obvious disgust reminded him of his mother and he felt ashamed. Ashamed because he'd spoilt a lady's midday walk. Ashamed because he'd so rarely pleased his mother. She'd have been disgusted at him, weeing in a field.

There was a burger van at the opposite end of the lay-by and the smell was divine: Ignatius hadn't eaten for eighteen hours. Nor had he had a drink or brushed his teeth. The inside of his mouth didn't feel pleasant. He imagined Maxine's response if she'd woken up next to him with his breath smelling like a sewer and his stomach sounding like an angry elephant. He checked in his pocket for change and headed over to the van.

"A large coffee and two bacon sarnies, please, mate."

The man behind the counter was in grease-spattered chef's whites. He nodded and placed more rashers on to fry. He buttered doorstep-size slices of bread and then turned the bacon over. He filled a cardboard mug with dark brown liquid and pressed a white plastic lid on to it.

"Sugar and milk are down the end of the counter," he said pushing the paper cup towards Ignatius. "Bacon'll be one minute."

Ignatius spooned sugar into his drink and added as much milk as possible without it slopping over the side of the cup. He stirred carefully and then drank. Despite the milk it was still slightly too hot, but after hours spent in that cramped car it felt like heaven to stand up straight in the autumn sunshine and taste strong, sweet coffee.

"That'll be £7.70," the chef said, dropping the sandwiches into two polystyrene boxes.

Ignatius put the coffee back on the counter and drew the money out of his pocket. There wasn't enough. He should have ordered only one sandwich but greed had got the better of him. There was Maxine's debit card, but this van didn't look the sort of place that took plastic.

"Sorry, mate, you got it wrong," he said. "I only ordered one sandwich."

"Two, you asked for two - definite."

Ignatius glanced at the chalked price list inside the van and counted out the exact money for one sandwich and one coffee. He placed it on the counter. Then he picked up one insulated box and headed back to the field without looking back at the man who'd served him.

The chef cursed in his wake. "What I am supposed to do with this other sandwich?"

Ignatius resisted the urge to tell him. Instead he looked for a bit of sunlit grass. Somewhere that didn't look damp and, if possible, was not sprinkled with rabbit poo. He eased his bulk down to the ground.

When he'd been on picnics as a child, his mother had always been prepared. There'd be a waterproof tarpaulin and then a blue and red checked blanket to lay over it to guard against cold bottoms. She'd bring a flask of milky coffee, ham sandwiches, loose tomatoes and homemade scones ready spread with jam. His father would sit and read the paper whilst she waxed lyrical about the benefits of the outdoors to a young boy. When they'd finished eating she'd produce a damp flannel that had been wrapped in tinfoil to retain the moisture. She'd use it to clean his face and wipe any last traces of jam from his fingers. Even when he reached his teens she'd insisted on doing this clean-up operation herself. She never quite trusted her son to do anything right.

He wasn't even allowed to travel to school by himself until after his father's death. All the other boys caught the bus to the grammar school. It was on that journey that friends were made, nicknames assigned and in-jokes evolved. But Ignatius's mother insisted that he be driven to school by his father on his way to work, excluding him from the camaraderie.

"You drive almost past the school, Geoffrey," she said when either he or his father tried to argue. "So what's the point in making Ignatius rush for the bus at some unearthly hour in the morning so he can spend the journey squashed among noisy, aggressive adolescent boys?"

Ignatius tried to fight his corner some days.

"But Mum …"

"Ignatius," she would interrupt, in the voice that insinuated he must be really stupid if he couldn't see the advantage of doing things her way. "Ignatius, it's far more productive and better for your future if you spend an extra few minutes here with me checking your homework, and then you can travel in comfort, reciting French verbs or the periodic table to your father, and arrive at school fresh and still looking smart. Some of those boys look like tramps when they get off the bus, and I'm sure their mothers didn't allow them to leave home like that."

Much to Ignatius's relief, his father never made him recite anything in the car, and they never let on to Winifred. They travelled in silence, each engrossed in his private thoughts. It had only been at his father's funeral that Ignatius realised his mother had made his father as miserable as him. But his father had been able to take comfort elsewhere.

The bacon sandwich was heavenly and Ignatius wished he'd had enough money for the second one. He wondered whether the chef had kept it warm to sell to someone else. He picked up the coffee. Savoury grease, followed by caffeine and sugar - what more could a man want for breakfast? He wiped his lips with the cheap serviette that had lined the polystyrene box. At his father's wake they'd had quality serviettes and a top of the range finger buffet.

"People will think badly of us if we don't put on a good spread," his mother had said.

On the same day, they'd discovered the house was only rented. Ignatius had admired his mother for marching on as though she'd been left well provided for. The only time she'd shown weakness was when that woman had crept into the crematorium chapel just as the service was about to get under way. Winifred had turned around just as she walked in. Her grip on Ignatius's hand had tightened.

"That damn woman!" she'd whispered. "How dare she show her face here?"

Then the minister had begun the service and there'd

been no time to ask what his mother had meant. Afterwards, the woman had stood some distance from the other mourners. She'd held a single red rose and appeared to be waiting for an opportunity to place it with the growing pile of tributes around the small sign indicating 'Geoffrey Smith'. As people started to drift off to their cars and the wake, Ignatius took a deep breath and approached her. His mother called him back but he ignored her. He might be only sixteen years old but he had a right to know certain things.

"I don't think we've met." There was a tremor in his voice and he felt his cheeks grow warm; he hated talking to strangers but this was for his father's sake. "I'm Ignatius, Geoffrey's son. Were you a friend of Dad's?"

Ignatius offered his hand as he'd seen his father do when introducing himself. The woman hesitated, her eyes flicked from Ignatius's face to his highly polished shoes and back again. Then she shook his hand.

"I …maybe I shouldn't be here … it's nice to meet you … he talked about you a lot." Her voice was shaky and her eyes were red from crying. "This is an odd situation. I don't know what he'd have wanted me to say."

He talked about you a lot. Ignatius had felt elated when the woman said those words. Even now, decades later, he still rolled them around his mind when he felt unloved. At the funeral the words had made him cry and he'd instantly liked the woman.

"I'm sorry. I've upset you," she said.

He'd pulled out the new handkerchief his mother had pressed on him that morning.

"It's fine," he sniffed. "Tell me how you knew him."

"We were close for many years. Very close."

That was when Ignatius guessed the truth. He should

71

have felt hurt at the betrayal but he wasn't even surprised.

"It's quietened down now, if you'd like to place your rose."

It was the least he could offer someone who had truly loved his father.

"Ignatius! Leave that woman. We're going to be late." His mother's voice was harsh.

"Please, go to your mother," said the woman. "I'll be fine."

He talked about you a lot. That was the treasure Ignatius had taken away from meeting his father's lover. He never saw her again.

The next day, curiosity drove Ignatius back to the crematorium after school. The floral tributes were still there. The single red rose was on top. He picked it up to read the card.

"To my darling Geoffrey, a man of principle and passion. Thank you for the time we spent together. Yours until we meet again, Veronica."

Ignatius removed the card and put it in his trouser pocket. He bent the rose in two and dropped it into a compost bin as he left the crematorium. When his mother returned to view the tributes there'd be no point in her becoming upset about something that no longer mattered.

Even now, sitting on the damp earth with an empty cardboard coffee cup in front of him, he found it comforting to know that his father had enjoyed some love and pleasure in a life otherwise dominated by a bossy, blinkered wife. Perhaps that's what had stopped his father cracking and losing control with Winifred. Maxine, in turn, had brought Ignatius love and pleasure, but five years too late to stop him losing control with his mother.

Ignatius headed back to his car, hoping the burger van chef wouldn't notice him.

Chapter Seven

"Dad, please can we call for Halifax? She likes going to the playground."

"You're a bit young to be starting with girls, aren't you?" Ian teased.

"It's not because she's a girl. It's because she's brave, especially on climbing frames and monkey bars. And none of my friends live near your flat and a playground's boring on your own."

Ian winced at the small criticism but was still tempted to refuse to invite Halifax on their outing. He'd enjoyed that mug of tea with Sandra earlier but he didn't want her to get the wrong idea if he kept turning up on her doorstep. And he didn't want Marcus telling Josephine about 'a girlfriend'.

"Please, Dad! And we have to go NOW because otherwise Mum will be here and then I'll have to go."

His son was right. Josephine had a late meeting at work and had called Ian to ask him to collect his son from school. He'd agreed like a shot. This was what he'd moved to Birmingham for: the chance to do normal 'dad' things with Marcus. It didn't matter that Josephine was using him to her advantage; it also meant his ex-wife was developing a measure of trust in him again.

Ian had stood proudly at the school gate waiting for his son. Marcus had come out with another boy and they'd raced across the tarmac playground towards the parents. The teacher was watching to make sure every child had an adult waiting. Her eyes had met Ian's just before he bent to hug Marcus. What followed had been embarrassing. She'd marched towards him, waving her arm to indicate that he should wait where he was. The other parents and grandparents stared as they set off home with their charges.

"Dad! What have you done?" hissed Marcus. "Miss Floyd only looks like that when something really bad's happened."

"Excuse me, sir." Miss Floyd was a little out of breath. "Ms Pilkington is the only adult approved to collect Marcus. I have the list of approved adults here and there's no man on it for Marcus."

Ms Pilkington? Marcus was taken aback. He hadn't realised that Josephine had reverted to her maiden name.

"He's my dad," said Marcus. "It's O.K."

"Even so, I'm going to have to phone Ms Pilkington for approval. Please come and wait inside."

Red-faced, Ian followed her. It was years since he'd been inside a school. He was surprised at how bright, airy and colourful everything was. Marcus took him on a tour of his artwork. The pictures had moved on since his son's finger-painted nursery offerings pre-divorce and Ian was careful to find a different praiseworthy sentence about each one.

"The colours in those flowers are spot on … Wow, a knight in armour! He looks terribly fierce!"

The teacher's phone call took a long time but Marcus was enjoying showing off to his dad. He fetched a red exercise book for him to look at. The last piece of work in it was from the previous day and was entitled "A Nice Thing Happened To Me".

It was written in pencil in a childish hand. The first two sentences brought a lump to Ian's throat.

"The best thing happened to me," read Ian. "My dad came to my house for tea. I have been to his bedsit too."

A rather lurid description of Ian's living arrangements followed but Ian didn't care if the teacher thought he was a tramp on a park bench. It was how his son felt that mattered, and that short essay gave Ian the impression that Marcus was happy with the situation. It had been worth moving north.

"All sorted!" Miss Floyd came back into the classroom smiling. "I've spoken to Ms Pilkington and she gave permission for you to take Marcus. I've got a form here that she needs to sign so we don't have to go through all this rigmarole next time. I'll pop it in Marcus's book bag so it won't get lost."

Now the book bag lay discarded on the scruffy dining table in the bedsit. Marcus had other things on his mind than reading, such as persuading his dad that Halifax should go to the playground with them.

"So, let's call for Halifax now. Before Mum comes," he repeated.

Ian gave in. Sandra could read into it what she wanted but he was only doing what was best for his son.

"Yes, let's."

Marcus knocked harder than was necessary on the scuffed door of bedsit two. Ian heard Sandra put the chain on before she opened it.

"Does Halifax want to go to the playground?" asked Marcus as soon as there was a gap big enough to speak through.

"I'm here too," said Ian, realising he wasn't visible to Sandra because Marcus was crowding the chained opening. "I'll keep an eye on her if you want to stay at home and cook supper."

He wanted her to know it was Halifax's company they were after, not hers.

"Tea," she said. "Around here we have tea, not supper."

"There's not much time before my mum's collecting me."

Marcus obviously wasn't going to stand for any game-playing by the adults.

"Yes, I do want to go!" Halifax's voice could be heard from within the flat.

"Love, you're going to Chelsea's sleepover later." Sandra's voice became muffled as she turned to talk to her daughter.

"That's not for ages. Please let me go, Mum!"

When they got to the playground a man was already sitting on the only bench, reading a newspaper. Sandra sat next to him. Ian sat next to her. There was just enough room without him having to squeeze close to her or pretend he'd rather remain standing. He felt awkward and didn't know what to say. The children were following each other up and down the slide, which seemed to have regained its slipperiness. It was easy to be natural together at that age. There was no trying to second-guess what the other wanted or was thinking. Children didn't worry about giving the wrong impression.

Sandra seemed to edge away from him. He wondered if she knew the man on her right. Now she was peering over his shoulder at the newspaper. Unless she knew him, it seemed the height of bad manners to invade someone's personal space like that.

"Look!" he said, to regain her attention. "Halifax and Marcus are coming down the slide together now."

He waved to the children and they waved back as they sailed down the slope, one immediately behind the other.

Sandra was oblivious.

Fed up of her bad manners, Ian wandered down to the pond. She was obviously more interested in the other chap. He wouldn't hang around being a gooseberry or cramping her style. When he looked back, the two of them were talking.

Ian fought an unexpected pang of jealousy. What did it matter what she did? She lived here and Ian would soon be gone. Hopefully over one of those bridges he was building towards Josephine. Sandra probably knew the man. He might be an ex-boyfriend. Perhaps he was Halifax's father. Ian looked at him again and decided he was too old.

"Ian!"

The man was walking away and Sandra was almost running over the grass towards him. She was clutching the newspaper.

"He let me keep his paper. Look here."

She was pointing at a story on page three of The Evening Mail. The headline was 'Missing Two Weeks'. The accompanying photograph was the girl in the armchair with the crossed out face. But this picture wasn't spoiled. The subject was laughing and fingering a miniature paper parasol hanging from the rim of a large cocktail glass.

"It's Maxine!" Sandra's voice was urgent. "It says she hasn't been seen at work or by her parents for two weeks. That's about when she and Ignatius left Vesey Villa. I spotted the picture over his shoulder and then talked him into giving me the paper. I said I knew the girl."

Ian took the paper. The story said that Maxine's mother had called the police when Pliable Plastics Ltd. had phoned to ask why her daughter hadn't turned up to work for nearly ten days; if Maxine didn't get in touch or provide a sick note she was in danger of disciplinary action or even losing her job. A description of Maxine followed. The article said she'd been staying with a boyfriend. The boyfriend, Ignatius Smith, also worked at Pliable Plastics. He couldn't be located, either.

"It's a bit suspicious, isn't it?" said Sandra. "Why would they both chuck in their jobs like that?"

"Perhaps they got a better offer elsewhere? It says the police are treating it as a simple missing persons' case. They don't seem to think it's suspicious."

"So why did he come back and try to break in?"

Ian shrugged. He was unnerved by what the newspaper report and Sandra were suggesting. But he pushed his unease aside. There were too many other things to sort out in Ian's life without wasting time on Maxine and her boyfriend. For a start, he was supposed to have bought a copy of the very paper Sandra had taken from the man on the bench, as part of his job-hunting strategy. Most professional recruitment was agency- and internet-based, but it was worth checking the paper. He returned it to his neighbour

"Could I have the Mail when you've finished with it? No rush. Read it over your tea first."

Sandra grinned at his emphasis on the word tea.

***

After tea Sandra helped Halifax pack an overnight bag

and then walked her round to the girl's best friend's house.

"I like sleeping at Chelsea's house," said Halifax as she skipped along in the near darkness. "She's got a cat. It's Halloween soon and Chelsea says I can go around and Tibbles can be a witch's cat. She's not black but we can pretend that as well. Perhaps she'll let me bring Marcus."

"Marcus might not be here for long," Sandra said carefully. She didn't want Halifax thinking that Marcus and Ian were going to be a permanent fixture in their lives. "Now, love, you be good for Chelsea's mum and dad or they won't invite you again. And go straight to sleep. It's school in the morning."

The bedsit felt too quiet without her daughter there. Sandra was at a loose end with no Halifax to cajole into bed and no ironing to finish.

The park man's Evening Mail was lying on the armchair where she'd dropped it. She scanned some of the other stories, but she kept going back to the report about Maxine and Ignatius. Why would they disappear like that? Maxine had talked about her mother and she didn't seem like the sort of girl who would up sticks without telling her mum. Sandra would be distraught if Halifax did that to her. Maxine's mum must be out of her mind with worry.

The newspaper report combined with the photos that Ian had found made the whole situation unsettling. Should she go to the police? Perhaps she and Ian could go together and take the stuff from the cardboard box as well. She picked up her key ready to go and ask him. Then she paused. They seemed to have been in each other's pockets all day. Would he think she was chasing him if she went around again?

He was a nice bloke and very easy on the eye. But he

was a lot older than her and he came from a different world. No doubt he'd be off back to that world shortly. So all things considered, they could never be a couple. And he probably wouldn't touch a girl like her with a bargepole anyway. So there'd be no harm in going to see him and asking if he'd consider going to the police station with her. Would there? Besides, he'd asked if he could have the newspaper after her.

She stated her mission as soon as he opened the door.

"I think we should go to go to the police. And we need to take the stuff from that cardboard box."

"Sit down," he said, closing the door behind her.

There was an open bottle of red wine on the table. He fetched a second glass, filled it and handed it to her without asking if she wanted a drink. Sandra felt this wouldn't be the right time to admit that she was more of a WKD girl; Blue, if there was a choice of flavours. She repeated her reason for the visit.

"So what do you think?"

"They don't usually investigate missing adults and the contents of the box don't indicate that anything nasty's happened - other than he took his annoyance out on the photos. I think the police will tell us to go away. Remember, the paper says they're treating it as a simple missing persons' case."

Sandra knew he was right about the missing persons bit. When her uncle had walked out on her aunt and disappeared, they'd shown no interest at all. But she didn't think Maxine's case was quite the same.

"But surely the stuff in that box shows he wasn't stable?"

"When my car was vandalised there was actual proof of a crime but the police never came. Why would they be interested in someone's forgotten belongings?"

His words made sense, and Ian was probably better qualified in these matters than her. So she let it go. She picked up the wine and took a sip. Her taste buds recoiled at the initial flavour and she wished it was a sweet alcopop. But she persevered, not wanting to appear a philistine. After a few mouthfuls it became tolerable and as she felt the alcohol hit her blood stream it became pleasurable.

"You knocked that back quickly." Ian refilled her glass and topped his own up.

Pace yourself, girl, Sandra thought. It's been a while since you've been out drinking and it's going straight to your head. Try and make intelligent conversation.

"So, which are you?" she asked. "Strictly or X-Factor?"

"Neither." He shook his head and smiled. "I just about know they're both TV programmes but that's as far as it goes. I prefer Borgen and Wallander, but with the subtitles, not Kenneth Branagh."

"I see."

Sandra didn't have a clue what he was talking about but she wasn't going to let on. She drank more wine and wondered if one glass of wine was equal to one WKD in price, alcohol or anything else. It was definitely agreeing with her.

"So why did you and your wife split up?"

"That's a rather personal question."

"I told you how Halifax was conceived and I hadn't even had any alcohol then."

"Fair point. She left me because I went with a prostitute on an overnight work trip to Amsterdam."

Sandra took a sharp breath.

"I can imagine that didn't go down too well. How did she find out?"

"One of the group I was with posted a stupid

82

comment on Facebook."

"I'm with your wife on this one."

"I've learned my lesson and I wouldn't have done it sober. But she won't forgive and forget."

"I don't blame her for not having nothing to do with you."

"I can understand and accept that." Ian's face was solemn and then it suddenly broke into a grin. "But I can't let the double negative go so easily!"

"What?"

He took her hand. A warning light went on somewhere in her wine-muddled brain but she ignored it.

"The first negative was 'not having'," he said using his other hand to point to her first finger. "And 'nothing' was the second one. Choose one or the other, but if you include them both in the same phrase they cancel each other out. It's a bit like maths: when you multiply a negative number by another negative number, the product is positive."

Sandra's brain felt as though it was swimming in foreign waters without a life vest. But it was a comfortable place to be. She liked Ian and he made her feel safe. She wasn't the one he'd cheated on, and he'd learned his lesson.

Now he was telling her more about Marcus and his voice was full of pride. She shuffled nearer to him and laid her head on his shoulder. It was ages since she'd done this without worrying how to impress the guy or wondering whether bed was the next step. Ian made her feel comfortable. Or was it the wine? She looked up at him. He was looking down at her. It was the easiest and most natural thing in the world for their lips to meet. Their arms wrapped around each other and Sandra felt she was falling into heaven. Her body was filled with golden warmth. She pressed closer to him and responded eagerly to his tongue.

Then Ian pulled away.

"I'm sorry, Sandra. That shouldn't have happened." The gap between them on the settee was massive now. "I shouldn't have led you on like that."

"But neither of us is with anyone else. What's the matter?"

Sandra's voice was small. She already knew the answer. She felt she'd cheapened herself. Sandra simply wasn't good enough for Ian Wolvestone. He could tolerate her as a neighbour and maybe even as the mother of his son's friend. But she was from the lower rungs of society. She could never match him in manners or class. He'd just told her she couldn't even talk in proper sentences.

"I've too much on my plate at the moment for complications." He was too polite to say she was too rough for him. "It's been a long day and I could do with an early night …"

Ian's last sentence tailed off but Sandra got the hint.

"I'll be off then."

Without waiting for a response she left.

Chapter Eight

Sandra was Ian's first conscious thought as he surfaced from sleep the next morning. There was a heavy weight of regret in his chest. He'd treated her badly the previous evening. That kiss should never have happened and seeing her off the premises so abruptly had been unforgivable. Guiltily, he poured some of the Sugar Puffs that she'd brought into a bowl. Sandra had been generous with what little she had and he'd pushed it all back in her face.

His mouth was full when his mobile rang. He chewed and swallowed quickly. There was no name against the number showing on the screen.

"Hello? Ian Wolvestone speaking."

"Sorry for the early call. I'm ringing about the CV you emailed to us yesterday."

Ian pushed the bowl of cereal away and sat up straight. This was good news. The caller explained that Copper Plate Computing was holding interviews that day in the centre of Birmingham.

"We're looking to strengthen our team of project managers and, on paper, it looks like you might have the skills we need."

The company had arranged several interviews for

later in the day, so the recruiter wanted Ian to take the 10:00 am slot.

"No problem," said Ian.

It gave him one hour to smarten himself up, drive into Birmingham, park and find the office block. This was his ticket out of Vesey Villa and would put him on the way to showing Josephine he could be a responsible member of society. He couldn't let this interview be a problem. He abandoned his breakfast and reached for his electric shaver.

Fifteen minutes later he was trying to check himself over bit by bit in the small cracked mirror, cursing that he'd forgotten his decision to replace it with something bigger and clearer. Piecing the reflections together in his mind, he thought he was passable. His suit had survived the move north fairly crease-free and the jacket hid his rushed attempt to iron a shirt.

The morning traffic had eased, giving him an easy run into the city centre. But parking was a problem because everywhere was already full of commuters. He was beginning to panic and considered abandoning the car on double yellow lines when he spotted a space on a parking meter. He pumped coins into the machine and headed into the office building across the road.

The receptionist offered him coffee. Ian refused; he didn't want to reveal his nerves by a cup rattling in its saucer or a spoon knocked to the floor. The leather and steel chairs in the waiting area were uncomfortable. It was almost ten o'clock. Ian tried to gather his thoughts. A brochure for Copper Plate Computing lay on the smoked glass coffee table to his right. Knowing nothing about the company, he picked it up.

He'd read only the first page when a man in a dark suit and a red tie approached. They shook hands. The man had a very tight grip.

"Ian Wolvestone? I'm James Hudson and I'm on the interview panel. Please come this way."

Two more men were seated at a boardroom table in the large interview room. James Hudson took a seat in the middle and gestured to Ian to sit opposite. Then he introduced his two colleagues and started the inquisition.

"It's good to have you with us, Ian. What do you know about Copper Plate Computing?"

Ian waffled about the short notice interview not giving him time to do much research.

"So you applied for a job without knowing anything about the company?" asked the man on the right. His jacket hung on the back of his chair and he looked more easy-going than the other two, but his words sent a barbed message.

"Websites can give the facts and figures about a company." Ian attempted to explain himself. "But only a visit can tell you about the culture, staff attitudes and the working atmosphere. So I don't base my applications on internet research. I believe it would narrow my options on inadequate evidence."

The three men nodded in unison.

"Tell us about your last job," the man on the left said. He was older than the other two and looked as though he wouldn't take any nonsense.

Ian emphasised the highlights, successes and promotions of his last post. It seemed to go down well. James Hudson glanced at the papers in front of him.

"And you were made redundant?"

"Yes."

Then Ian was invited to ask questions and his lack of preparation let him down again. He could make only generalised queries. As James Hudson showed him out, Ian knew he'd failed. If he was to get out of Vesey Villa and make the right impression on Josephine, he'd have to make job hunting into a career in its own right.

Back at the bedsit he spent the afternoon emailing CVs to recruitment agencies and trawling the websites of all the large Midlands-based companies. At four o'clock his mobile rang.

"Dad! It's me, Marcus. We're on our way to yours and I'm staying overnight!"

"What? That's great!"

Ian's mood lifted instantly at his son's excitement.

Josephine must need a short-notice babysitter, but she'd obviously accepted that Marcus loved seeing his dad and Vesey Villa wasn't such a bad place after all. Ian didn't care what had prompted the visit. Marcus was coming and that was all that mattered.

"Mum's going to her Reading Group. She wanted to ask Aunty Carole to babysit. She's not really an aunty, she's mum's friend. But I said I wanted to come to you. We had a bit of an argument but I won. We've just been home from school to fetch my pyjamas and we'll be at yours in …"

"Fifteen minutes," Josephine called.

"Fifteen minutes, Mum says."

"Sugar Puffs O.K. for breakfast? And I've got Millionaire's Shortbread from our old neighbour, Mrs Drinkwater. She gave it to me when I moved out and I forgot about it last time you came."

"Brilliant!"

Ian ended the call and smiled to himself. Then he remembered Marcus's enthusiasm for playing with Halifax in the park. His guilty feelings about the way he'd treated Sandra returned. What if his son insisted on calling for Halifax and going to the playground again this afternoon? Last night's kiss would make things awkward and embarrassing. Ian was ashamed. Seven days earlier he wouldn't have gone anywhere near a young, single mother living on the poverty line in a bedsit. Yet the kiss last night had seemed so natural, and it had been toe-curling.

It had been a long time since he'd been physically close to a woman. Since the divorce he'd had a couple of pathetic attempts at internet dating but neither had been enjoyable. Both women had been too desperate to find love. Despite the huge chasm between them, Sandra's company was enjoyable. Last night he'd wanted to keep her in his arms, but the sharp cold voice of reason had insisted that he do the honourable thing and let her go. A long-term future for them wasn't viable, so he shouldn't tease her with the fantasy.

Ian looked out of the window. The sky was grey and it was beginning to rain. It was too wet for the playground so he could put off seeing Sandra for a little longer.

***

Ignatius drove up to the top deck of the multi-storey car park. He stopped at the spot from where his mother had fallen. No trace of her had been found up here, but the police had calculated the spot from which she'd tumbled. Ignatius knew they'd got their sums right.

He got out of the car into the drizzle. This was where he felt closest to her. The crematorium plaque citing both his parents gave some comfort, but it was here that he felt his mother's spirit. Perhaps that's because the dead leave something of their soul behind at the place where they took their last breath, especially if they were terrified at the time.

Ignatius pulled up his overcoat collar and fastened the stiff top button. There was a chilly breeze here that wasn't apparent down below. He headed to the concrete kiosk near the 'down' ramp. He'd discovered this small abandoned building during one of his many visits in the immediate aftermath of his mother's death. Sometimes he brought a flask of coffee and some sandwiches in here. There was a wooden bench in the kiosk. There he'd sit out of the wind and pick through his memories. Once the door was closed, reality receded and it was easy to travel back in time.

He talked about you a lot. That was one of his best memories. Another very good one was the day the letter arrived offering him a place at grammar school. Mother had thrown caution to the wind and he'd been granted his wish to visit Drayton Manor Park. They'd taken a picnic with hunks of homemade chocolate cake.

The day his mother died, the weather had been lovely. It was spring and there'd been a feeling of optimism in the air. Even Ignatius had felt good that day, as though he was about to do something that would improve his life. And mostly it had.

It was her Bridge Club evening. She walked there during the summer when the weather was fine but always insisted that Ignatius collect her in the car because she didn't consider it safe, or the 'done thing', for a lady to walk home alone in the dark.

"You will be there at 10 o'clock on the dot, won't you?" she'd confirmed as she picked up her handbag and checked her purse. "Set off a few minutes early to make sure."

She never let him forget the one occasion he'd been ten minutes late. He'd left home in plenty of time but there'd been an accident and a road had been closed. Consequently, all the way back his mother had lectured him about how he should have allowed time for unforeseen mishaps.

The quickest route home from the Bridge Club took them past the multi-storey car park. More than once his mother had glanced up at its darkened levels. As part of a council money-saving initiative most of the lights went off in the early evening when the car park emptied of commuters. Only the stairwell was lit twenty-four hours a day.

"It wouldn't surprise me if there's a murder up there one of these days. What a God-forsaken, spooky place when it's dark. It would be a terrible place to breathe your last."

So on that positive warm evening, as he drove his mother home and she rattled on about his inadequacies and failings, the car park was the place Ignatius chose to start turning his life around. He did it on impulse. A light went on in his brain telling him he didn't have to put up with this anymore.

"Where are we going?" she'd asked. There was a faint trace of panic in her voice when he turned into the car park.

"I thought you might like to see the view from the top. We can look down on the colourful lights of the city. It's like a free illuminations show."

"Don't be silly, Ignatius. If I want to see illuminations I'll put my name down for the Women's Institute coach trip to Blackpool. Take me home."

By that time, the car was crawling up the concrete slope to the second floor. Ignatius had been surprised the place wasn't locked up at night. But it was open and he was going to take advantage of it. It wasn't a residential area and the few businesses around had closed hours ago. Even the burger bar opposite the car park was shut that evening. There was no nightlife in this part of town.

"Let's just see the view. We've never been up here in

the dark before."

"You need your head examining, Ignatius. Who in their right mind drives into a pitch black multi-storey car park when they're not looking for a parking space? I knew there was something wrong with you from the moment you were born. But I've always done my best to protect and guide you. And what thanks do I get? I'll be making you an appointment at the doctor's tomorrow and I'll be coming with you to make sure he gets the right tale. I should've pushed for some proper treatment when you had that breakdown. All they did was talk to you and give you a few pills."

"I don't think you'll be doing anything tomorrow."

"Since when did you tell me what I would and wouldn't be doing?"

Ignatius said nothing.

The headlights ran along the concrete barricade on the seventh floor. Ignatius guided the car round and then up the final ramp to the eighth. He pulled up in the middle of the deck and switched off the headlights. There was no point in drawing attention. He walked round and opened the passenger door.

"Come on. Time to survey the city."

"You go if you want. I'm staying here." She'd been sitting stiffly, clutching her navy Margaret Thatcher style handbag on her lap. "But hurry up! It's cold and I'm tired."

Now, in the teatime drizzle, he left the kiosk and walked to the centre of the deck where he'd parked five years ago. At this time of day only a handful of cars remained up here. He doubted whether the top deck ever got full. People couldn't be bothered to manoeuvre all the way up.

He remembered how he'd almost had to manhandle his mother out of the car. In the end he'd put his hand over her mouth because she was making too much noise. Then he'd found an old handkerchief in his pocket and had stuffed it between her lips. The silence had given him space to collect his thoughts.

He'd been careful not to grip her wrists too hard as he propelled her to the edge. He didn't want to leave bruises or any other marks that would indicate another person's involvement in her death. As they stood looking towards the bright lights of the city centre, Ignatius had asked if she'd be happy to write a suicide note. They could leave it under a stone near where they stood. He'd taken the glove box 'emergency' pen and paper from the car. She'd shaken her head violently, unable to speak because of the handkerchief, and then she'd retched as though she was about to be sick. She'd even tried to kick him with her neat little court shoes.

Now, standing in the damp October air, he pulled a pair of gloves from the pockets of his overcoat and decided that autumn had definitely arrived. He didn't regret the action he'd had to take over his mother, but when the going got tough he missed her. She'd never allowed him any freedom, but never having freedom meant he'd never had to take responsibility. Life had been easier then.

His mother's death couldn't have been described as peaceful. The undertaker had described it as 'sudden' in the death notice for the local paper. The notice had been pointless since the full story of his mother's mysterious fall/jump was all over the press already. But the undertaker insisted on posting the notice because it was part of the funeral package.

At the last minute on that warm evening, and with no warning, he'd yanked the handkerchief from her mouth and pushed her firmly in the back. There'd been just one scream as she'd toppled over the barricade and then a thump as she hit the ground.

Ignatius had raced back to the car and driven down the eight concrete slopes quickly but carefully. If he'd left even a scrape of paint on one of the concrete pillars, it would have placed him at the scene and brought him under suspicion. He'd been back home, his breathing steady, when the police knocked on the door with news of his mother's death.

"It's my fault!" he'd exclaimed and burst into tears.

The policewoman had tried to calm him and someone else produced hot sweet tea.

"I always collect her from Bridge club. I wait in the church hall car park until she comes out. But tonight she said not to come. She said there was a new member who lived near us and she'd offered Mum a lift."

The police had come back several times and once or twice the questions had become rather awkward. Ignatius had no alibi. Several people had said he didn't seem mentally balanced. A Bridge club member who left early thought she'd seen Ignatius's car waiting outside the church hall but she couldn't swear to it.

In the end his mother's death had received an open verdict. Many of his mother's friends didn't agree with it but there'd been no evidence to the contrary.

"He'll kill again!" one of the neighbours had shouted to the press on the steps of the coroner's court.

"There's something wrong with Winifred's son!" his mother's Bridge partner had insisted at the wake, when she thought Ignatius was out of earshot. "Next time it might be a complete stranger in the street, like these 'care in the community' cases who walk around city centres stabbing people."

But Betty had always had absolute faith in him. "Any fool can see you were devoted to her. I'd be proud to have you as my son." That was another phrase Ignatius stored away with 'he talked about you often'.

It was starting to rain properly now. Ignatius touched the concrete barrier; it was the last thing to hold his mother's fingerprints. He wished he'd asked her for a cuddle before she went. As he'd become an adult, that's what he'd missed - the few occasions of physical closeness with his mother. They'd chased away his night terrors and the pain of being shunned by the other children at school. But he had to be good to earn those cuddles. Often, if he'd failed in some way, he was left to cry all night.

Of course Maxine had cuddled him, but not in the protective, maternal way that he craved.

Now there was no one to administer comfort. Perhaps it was time to find someone else. He needed someone who'd love him without criticising, as his dead son would have done.

***

Halifax was hopping up and down trying to look over the counter in the police station as they waited to be seen.

"Is this a proper police place? Like on the TV, Mummy?"

"Shhhh!" Sandra bent towards her daughter and put her finger on her lips. "Yes, it is a proper police place and you must be quiet so Mummy can talk to the policeman."

"What are you going to talk about, Mummy? Have you ..."

Sandra turned to Halifax again and gave her a 'you are being naughty' look. The little girl fell quiet and went back to hopping from foot to foot.

Maxine's disappearance, the newspaper report and

the cardboard box had been playing on Sandra's mind since the previous evening, possibly because she didn't want to think about what had really upset her: the way Ian had dismissed her after a kiss that must have made his toes curl as much as her own. After that rebuff she couldn't ask him again to go with her to the police station, so here she was alone and without the photos or the scrapbook to add weight to her argument.

"Can I help you?"

The uniformed policeman looked very young, even to Sandra.

"I've got concerns about an ex-tenant in the building where I live."

"What sort of concerns?"

Sandra told him how Ignatius and Maxine seemed to have moved out in a big hurry and about the cardboard box that Ian had found in his wardrobe.

"The photos are what spooked me," she said. "There's a big red cross scrawled across the girl's face as though whoever drew it wanted her dead. And now she's disappeared. Neither her work nor her parents have seen her for a couple of weeks."

"I see," said the policeman.

"I think she might be dead," Sandra whispered the last word so that Halifax couldn't hear.

"That's very informative. We'll look into it."

The policeman looked up from his form-filling and smiled.

"Is that it?" Sandra asked.

"Yes, that's it."

"Don't I get to go into an interview room with a tape recorder and coffee in a paper cup?"

"We save that treat for suspects. We'll be in touch if we need more information. I've got your mobile number."

Chapter Nine

"Can we get chips, Dad?" Marcus asked as soon as Josephine had dropped him at the bedsit. "Mum never lets us have chips."

"Yes, chips can be our Friday night treat. There's a chip shop just down the road. Let's wait a bit, though. It's raining."

"So what shall we do now, Dad?"

Marcus wandered around the room, picking things up, putting them down, opening cupboard doors and looking in dark corners. "Have you got an Xbox?"

"Not yet. What about that Top Trumps game you brought last time? I think you left it behind somewhere."

Ian started rummaging in the pile of newspapers and junk mail that had already accumulated on the table. Finally he unearthed the pack of cards. They played a couple of games but Marcus was half-hearted. He kept walking around the room and staring out of the window as though he was full of unspent energy.

"Do you fancy a piece of Mrs Drinkwater's Millionaire's shortbread?" Ian suggested. "And the rain's just about stopped so we could have a quick kick around in the garden before we get those chips."

Marcus gave his attention to nibbling the chocolate from the top of the shortbread. Then he licked the toffee and finally bit into the shortbread base.

"Does Mum let you eat like that?" Ian asked as his son licked his forefinger and dabbed it on the plate to gather every last crumb.

"We never have Millionaire's Shortbread at home. But if we did I expect she'd want me to eat it nicely. That's why I like coming here, you don't care so much about doing things properly."

"You'll get me shot! Now fetch the football. It's behind the settee somewhere. Let's go outside."

"It's a shame Buster's not here. He likes football. I hope Mum remembers to walk him before she goes to her book group."

The air was damp and autumnal. Ian had surveyed the back garden of Vesey Villa from his window but he'd never been in it. He couldn't find an accessible back door from the house so he took Marcus out the front and they located a side gate that led to the back.

Marcus put the ball down and kicked it across the lawn. It hit the side of a dilapidated shed and then rolled back towards him.

"Careful!" Ian warned. "I don't think that thing can take much battering. Kick it to me."

For several minutes they passed the ball back and forth. Marcus took great delight in sending it just out of his dad's reach so Ian had to run for it. It felt good to be outside, running around with his lad.

"I'm going to be King of the Castle!" Marcus abandoned the ball and ran up a hillock of bare earth. "I'm higher than you!"

Ian chased Marcus up the hill and rugby tackled his son to the ground. Then he realised his mistake. They were both covered in soil and mud.

Ian stood and brushed himself down.

"I hope Mum packed some spare clothes for you?"

"Probably."

Marcus was running along the hillock his arms outstretched making aeroplane noises. "There's a funny smell around here. Is it you, Dad?"

"No it is not!" Ian gave his son a gentle punch. "I thought it was you polluting the atmosphere."

As Marcus flew his pretend plane backwards and forwards along the freshly-dug hillock, Ian wondered who'd been digging the garden. Sandra didn't seem the gardening sort and it was unlikely to be the prostitute from upstairs. That only left the ground floor tenant.

Sandra had told him that the ground floor flat was twice as big and twice as expensive as the others. It had a separate bedroom and its own bathroom. An old lady lived there and sometimes the district nurse visited her and left one of those yellow clinical waste bags out the front. A sick elderly woman wouldn't have been gardening, either. Perhaps the landlord had got a gardener to give the place a makeover.

Marcus revved his engine up loudly and soared down the hill, around the lawn and into Ian's arms.

"I'm hungry," he announced.

***

Ignatius had parked beside the Golden Swan again. He liked being in a familiar place and no one had yet grown suspicious of him or the car. He'd chosen a spot that was partly obscured by overgrown bushes but still gave him a view of the comings and goings at Vesey Villa. Getting the cardboard box back was his number one priority. Without Maxine, life had become lonely and he was desperate to see Teddy Bear again. And there was the pregnancy test, the only thing he had to remind him of the son that never was. The boy would've been his only living relative. The boy would've loved him. It was probably fanciful, but he liked to think that that white stick held the DNA of the boy who might have become his descendent. Perhaps one day the baby could even be cloned from the pregnancy test and then Ignatius could leave a proper legacy to the world.

He willed the new tenant to walk out of the front door so he could walk in. Instead, the purple-haired girl went into the house with her daughter. The little one was holding a pink helium balloon. She had to tug it down in order to get through the front door.

Maxine had been fond of the little girl. She'd bought sweets specifically to hand out to her. Maxine liked children, other people's children. They'd never discussed it, but Ignatius had assumed that all women wanted kids. He wanted a son. He needed a son, a little boy he could turn into the man he'd failed to become. If he could make his son a successful, confident member of society, it would be almost as good as if he'd become that person himself. It would make Mother proud.

When Maxine had told him about the positive pregnancy test he'd been excited.

"How soon before we know if it's a boy or girl?"

"I don't want it," she'd said, and burst into tears. "I'd be absolutely no good as a mum."

Ignatius couldn't understand the female hysterics.

"That's O.K. If it's a boy I'll keep it. I'll look after him for you."

He imagined a well-behaved little boy growing into an academically strong teenager and then becoming a doctor, lawyer or politician.

"And if it's a girl?" she sobbed.

He paused. Women were a foreign country to him.

"You can keep it. I don't understand females."

"You are mental. You can't choose to love a baby of one sex but not the other."

YOU ARE MENTAL. Maxine stopped speaking but the words were seeking out the dark corners of his brain.

YOU ARE MENTAL. The words were stabbing at him.

YOU ARE MENTAL. The words the sixth form bullies had used.

YOU ARE MENTAL. His mum had said it when he'd abandoned his A' levels.

YOU ARE MENTAL. YOU ARE MENTAL. YOU ARE MENTAL.

"Don't say those words!"

He'd raised his arms and moved towards her. He wanted to kill her.

She'd dodged him and run from the flat.

"You are mental. No way can I have your baby!"

She'd headed for the stairs. He'd sat down, shaking. He was glad she'd escaped. If he'd hurt her he might have hurt his unborn son. She'd left the pregnancy test on the table. He'd picked it up and stared at the blue line. A blue line: that must mean it was a boy, otherwise the line would've been pink. Why hadn't she said it was a boy? He wanted her back. He wanted the son she was carrying.

She didn't come back that night, or the next, or the one after that. Ignatius worried about his unborn son. A son's place was with his father.

A week later, Maxine tapped on the door. He knew it was her but he didn't answer. She put her key into the lock. When she opened the door he was sitting in the armchair, facing her. She let out a gasp.

"I thought you'd be at work. I just came to get my stuff."

She was scared, which was the way he wanted it.

"I haven't been to work. I've been waiting for you and my son to come back. You can stay here until he's born and then you can leave. Mothers aren't good at bringing up boys."

She looked pale and tired.

"Have you been taking care of him? No drinking?"

"The baby's gone," she muttered, moving around the room picking up her belongings.

"Gone? What do you mean, 'gone'?"

He stood over her as she pushed clothes into a series of supermarket carrier bags.

"I've had an abortion. Privately. Mum helped me out with the money."

He pushed her and she fell against the wall.

"You've murdered my son?"

His voice was vicious. Maxine struggled upright again.

"It wasn't your son. It was a cluster of cells. It wasn't a baby. It was nothing! It might have been a girl!"

"You murdered my son," he repeated and pushed his face into hers, grabbing her by the neck of her hoody. "You know what it says in the Bible, don't you?"

She shook her head. A tear crawled from one eye.

"An eye for an eye and a tooth for a tooth."

Now there was a tear in the other eye too. It served her right if she was upset.

"You murdered my son so now I'm going to kill you."

She yelped like a wounded puppy. He placed his hands on her throat.

"You are mental!"

She kicked him hard on the shins and he almost lost

his grip. He stamped on her toes. She screamed. He kept his left hand on her throat and punched her mouth with his right. Then he placed both hands on her neck and squeezed. And squeezed. And squeezed.

"Please! No!" Her whisper was hoarse.

He squeezed for a very long time. She stopped struggling. She became floppy.

He let go and stepped backwards. She crumpled to the floor.

"Serves you right," he'd hissed.

Then he'd gone to wash his hands and make a cup of tea. As he poured boiling water on to the teabag he began to tremble. He added extra sugar. Hot sweet tea was good for shock. It was what the policewoman had made for him when they came to tell him about Mother. It was the shock of learning that his unborn son had been murdered by its mother that was making him tremble now.

For a long time he'd sat with his back to Maxine's body, staring at the pregnancy test. It was the only thing he had of his son. It was the only thing to prove the boy had ever existed. Finally he'd gone to bed. He'd thrown Maxine's coat over her body so he wouldn't be constantly reminded of her treachery.

Now, in the Golden Swan car park, Ignatius shifted his legs around in the passenger foot well. Already he was stiff with cold and it wasn't yet fully dark. He must find somewhere proper to stay or he'd die of hypothermia. When all this had started a couple of weeks ago the weather had been much warmer.

He'd noticed the heat particularly on the morning after Maxine died. He'd woken early and there'd been a smell. He wondered if there was a problem with the shared bathroom but then he realised it came from somewhere closer. A couple of flies buzzed around the room. He'd tried to ignore the smell and sink back into the security of sleep, but before slumber took him again the events of the previous evening bludgeoned his mind.

Maxine's legs were sticking out from under her coat.

He sat up and tried to think what to do. She couldn't stay here. He couldn't take her anywhere in the daylight. How did they dispose of bodies on the TV? What would Mother have done?

"Mother wouldn't have killed a lady," said Teddy Bear from his position on Ignatius's pillow. "You should go to the police and own up. Owning up is always the best thing."

"No it isn't!" Ignatius retorted. "Owning up to spilling lemonade on the carpet is not the same thing as confessing to the police and being put away for life."

"Mother believed the punishment should fit the crime." Teddy Bear's glass eyes were unwavering. "That's why she poured water in your bed when you spilled the lemonade."

"Hanging was banned years ago."

"So go to the police. You'll never sleep at night if you don't confess."

Angry, Ignatius had jumped out of bed and pulled the cardboard box from his wardrobe. He'd saved it because Cheese and Onion crisps were his favourite flavour. He stuffed Teddy Bear and the pregnancy test inside on top of his mum's scrapbook.

Then he vented his anger on the two snapshots of Maxine that she'd pinned to the wall above his bed. He tore them down and grabbed the nearest writing implement, a red felt tip that Maxine had used to complete those silly word searches. He drew a big cross over her face in each picture and then stuffed them both into the box as well. He pushed it back in the wardrobe and, with Teddy, Maxine and Mother all unable to taunt him, his brain began to clear.

The obvious and easiest burial ground was right here in the back garden of Vesey Villa. He'd never seen a soul there except the old man the landlord paid to mow the lawn. Ignatius had bumped into him the other day as the man was loading his mower into the back of a small green van.

"That's me finished for the year," he'd said. "Some people cut all year round, but not me. It gets too wet in the winter. I'll be putting my feet up 'til March. Now I've got my pension coming in I can do as I fancy."

Ignatius had hardly acknowledged the man at the time, but it was very useful to know that no one would be going in the garden for months. By then the worms would've finished Maxine off. He planned to bury her after dark.

But he had to throw Maxine's mother off the trail. If she reported Maxine missing, the police would be round with their dogs and he'd be straight in the frame for murder. Somewhere, Maxine had some silly flowery notelets she'd bought in a sale because they were pretty. She'd liked wasting money.

"Who do you ever write to?" he'd mocked.

She'd been cross and had immediately sat down and written a note to her mother and then one to her best friend. He'd watched her copy the addresses in round handwriting from the little book she kept in her handbag.

Now he could do the same thing. He would write that he and Maxine had decided to go away for a while to mend their relationship. Her mother knew about the abortion so he couldn't pretend everything was hunky-dory between him and her daughter. His handwriting wouldn't match hers but he'd got a solution to that.

The notelets were in the drawer that Maxine had used for her underwear.

"Dear Maxine's Mum," he wrote, wondering if he'd ever known the woman's Christian name. "She's busy packing and asked me to tell you that we're going away to mend our relationship. If it works we may move permanently. Maxine and I will let you have the new address when we have somewhere proper to live. Best wishes, Ignatius."

He copied the same wording on to her friend Amy's card and then addressed the envelopes using the little book in Maxine's bag. It was a shame he didn't have Amy's surname. 'Amy' on the envelope would have to do.

Then he pushed the remaining notelets into the Cheese and Onion crisp box along with the address book. It would be a good idea to send another card in a few weeks' time to make sure they stayed off the scent. After that he'd packed up all Maxine's stuff and his stuff into separate bags and boxes and driven Maxine's things to Derby. The two of them had stopped to eat there on their way back from the Peak District when Maxine had insisted they have a day out for her birthday. Ignatius distributed her clothes, shoes and other paraphernalia around as many different charity shops as he could. He'd posted the cards at the same time so the postmarks would confuse the recipients. He was still rather proud of that touch.

Now, in the car, the evening was getting colder by the second. He wriggled around in the front passenger seat again to get his circulation flowing.

He'd covered up well after Maxine's death. There hadn't been a single policeman sniffing around Vesey Villa. Mother would be proud.

There was the story in the Evening Mail about

Maxine going missing but it didn't say she was dead. When Ignatius retrieved his cardboard box, he'd write another flowery card and post it directly to the police station from Derby. It would say that, after reading the newspaper report, Maxine just wanted to let them know she was alive and well. She was making a new life for herself with Ignatius and didn't want to be tracked down.

Despite his wriggling, Ignatius was as stiff as a board. He needed a walk. There was no one around and it wouldn't hurt to check the grave.

As he walked on to the forecourt of Vesey Villa he noticed Betty's yellow clinical waste sack. He wondered what happened to the sacks when they were taken away. Did anyone look inside them or were they simply incinerated? The old lady's sacks were never full; they were all floppy at the top - plenty of space to sneak in something extra. It might be possible to pop an arm in here or a leg in there.

Ignatius eased the garden gate open and then closed it behind him. The hillock of earth was just as he remembered it. No one had been digging there, animal or human.

A cloud slid away from the moon and the light in the garden brightened.

There were footprints in the soft earth. Ignatius didn't remember walking on the mound. He'd flattened it down with the spade as much as he could and then he'd scarpered. Besides, it had rained a few times since then. Wouldn't any prints of his have been washed away? The footprints were of two sizes, an adult and a child. The only youngster in the house belonged to the purple-haired woman.

He stood back and looked up at the house. All the curtains were closed but lights were still on. Something tickled in Ignatius' throat and he coughed. He coughed again and then fumbled in his pocket for a handkerchief to put over his mouth and muffle the sound.

The curtain moved in his old flat.

Chapter Ten

"There's someone out there, Daddy. I heard him cough." Marcus was sitting on the bed in his pyjamas, another half-nibbled piece of Millionaire's Shortbread in his hand. He was working on the toffee layer. "Why is somebody in the garden at night?"

Ian moved the curtain and looked down. It was pitch black. With the bedsit light on it was impossible to see anything outside. Then Ian heard the cough too. It sounded like someone banished to the garden for a smoke.

"Is it a burglar, Dad?" Marcus was staring up at him, wide-eyed.

"Turn the light out so I can see properly."

Marcus reached over and flicked the switch by the bed. Ian stared out of the window, waiting for his eyes to adjust. He tried to pick reality out of the shadows. At first he saw nothing but the dark blobs of bushes and the shed that Marcus had whacked the ball against. He was about to drop the curtain back into place when he saw movement. A figure was kicking at the loose soil on the freshly-dug mound. Then whoever it was stopped and walked around the hillock. His head was down as though he was examining the earth. The dark silhouette was stocky, like the man who'd tried to get into his flat, but Ian couldn't be sure it was the same person. The man kicked the earth again, seemed satisfied with the result, and went back towards the side of the house. Ian heard a faint thud as the gate closed.

"O.K. You can put the light back on now."

Ian let the curtain drop.

"So who was coughing?" asked Marcus, nibbling on the shortbread.

"No one. The noise must have come from one of the other bedsits. Haven't you finished eating that yet?"

"Nearly."

Ian watched his son enjoy the last mouthfuls of the sticky sweet shortbread. There was no point in scaring him with a tale of a man in the garden at this time of night. It was Ian's job to worry about the prowler.

"Toilet and teeth time."

"I can go on my own," said Marcus as Ian picked up his keys.

"It's getting late. I'll come with you."

Josephine was right. Vesey Villa was no place for a young boy to be walking about alone in his pyjamas, especially if there might be clients visiting the top floor flat and a prowler lurking.

Marcus fell asleep in two seconds flat but Ian struggled. He'd created a makeshift bed on the settee but it wasn't adequate for a grown man. His mind was buzzing with thoughts of Ignatius Smith and the prowler. Were they one and the same? Should Ian go to the police? It was several hours before sleep finally claimed him.

The hammering on the door started in his dream. When it became reality, Ian leapt off the settee.

"One minute!"

He pulled on his jeans and grabbed the sweatshirt

110

he'd worn the previous day. The sound of fist banging on wood continued.

"Dad?" Marcus mumbled as he came to. "What's going on?"

Ian looked at his watch. It was eight a.m.

"Nothing. You snuggle back down."

There was another, loud, forceful thump. Ian opened the door. Two uniformed police officers strode past him into the bedsit.

"I'm Sergeant Tetley and this is Constable Lisle," said the elder of the pair. They both produced identity cards. "We're following up reports about a young woman who's gone missing from this flat. We've been told there's incriminating evidence in a cardboard box in here."

Still befuddled with sleep, Ian struggled to marshal his thoughts. Two policemen in his flat at this time on a Saturday was surreal. He'd thought Sandra was the only other person who knew about the box.

"Dad?"

The officers appeared momentarily confused when they noticed Marcus sitting wide-eyed and open-mouthed on the bed.

"Who's this?"

Ian moved to stand between them and Marcus. "My son. That missing girl is nothing to do with me. You need to speak to the previous tenant."

Ian was feeling uncomfortable. This police visit wasn't going to go down well with Josephine. When Marcus eventually told her, she'd refuse any more overnight stays and perhaps even daytime access. All the bridges he thought he'd built between them would disintegrate. And what about Marcus? If he saw his father as a criminal he too might want nothing more to do with him.

The sergeant consulted his notebook.

"We need to speak to Ignatius Smith."

"That's not me. It's the previous tenant."

"Dad, I need the toilet."

"I need to see to my son," Ian said as forcefully as he dared. "You'll have to leave. I can't help you."

"We need a statement from you." The sergeant barred the bedsit door. "It'll be easier to do it at the station without ... your son."

"O.K." Ian concentrated on keeping his voice calm and agreeable. He didn't want Marcus to sense his unease. "I'll take him to his mother's and then come to the police station to make a statement."

"You're not going anywhere, sir. We'll ensure that the boy gets safely to his mother's house. Just give us the address."

Reluctantly, Ian did as they asked. Josephine would blow her top when the police turned up outside her front door with Marcus and her level of trust in him would plummet.

The constable called for another car to be sent to Vesey Villa.

"He needs some privacy to get dressed," said Ian, trying to make things as easy for his son as possible. "Let him take his clothes to the bathroom."

Ian gathered Marcus's belongings.

"Come on, lad," said the oldest of the officers kindly. "Show me where this bathroom is and then we'll get you home to Mum. Don't worry about Dad. He'll be fine with us."

Ian was allowed to get dressed properly too. Then they went downstairs to the waiting police cars. He felt a firm hand on his head as he ducked into the back seat. Through the window he watched Marcus being guided into the other car. There'd been no tears. His son was coping well.

At the police station it became apparent that they didn't believe he wasn't Ignatius Smith. The officers kept referring to his missing girlfriend, Maxine. Somewhere along the way they'd got hold of the wrong end of the stick.

"Do you have any photographs of her?" one of the officers asked.

"I'm not Ignatius Smith," Ian repeated once again.

The police looked sceptical. Ian fingered his collar and let his tongue slide over his top front teeth. This had to be Sandra's doing. It might be her way of getting back at him for the rotten way he'd treated her after that kiss. He didn't blame her.

"There are two photos of the girl in my flat," he said. "Someone has drawn a red cross on her face in felt tip pen. My driving licence is in the bedsit, too. It will prove I'm NOT Ignatius Smith."

They left him alone for a while with a Styrofoam cup of revolting coffee. It was the first drink he'd had since being pulled from his bed, so he drank it.

The man who'd taken Marcus home came into the room.

"Terrible, isn't it?" He pointed at the coffee. "That machine gets worse by the day."

Ian gave a brief nod of his head.

"Your wife was shocked when we turned up on her doorstep."

"Ex-wife," Ian corrected.

"That's a grand lad you've got there. He was as happy as Larry to be in a police car and not scared at all. He wanted us to put the blue lights on. We couldn't do that without proper reason. But when we'd stopped at your wife's house -"

"Ex-wife," Ian interrupted.

"Ex-wife, sorry. I stuck the lights on for a minute without the sirens while my colleague rang the doorbell."

"So Josephine woke up to see her son sitting in a police car with the blue light on?"

"It was a shock for her at first but once she realised that he wasn't harmed or in any trouble she calmed down. She had a few choice words to say about you, though!"

"That's not difficult to imagine."

Eventually the police drove Ian back to the bedsit. As they walked up the stairs, Sandra and Halifax emerged.

"Oh my God!" Sandra put her hand to her mouth when she saw him flanked by two police officers. "Ian! I didn't think … have you been arrested? I am so sorry!"

"It's O.K." Ian could see that her distress was genuine. "I think we've nearly cleared up the case of mistaken identity. They thought I was Ignatius."

"I am so sorry," she repeated. "I was worried about Maxine."

"At least I'm not handcuffed."

He gave her a little wave with both hands. The police hustled him past Sandra's door and into his flat. Ian went straight to the wardrobe and got out the cardboard box. He handed them the photographs. One of the men put gloves on and dropped the pictures into an evidence bag.

"I think it might be a bit late for that," said Ian. "Sandra and I have both touched them."

"Can I take the box, sir?"

It felt like a weight lifted from his shoulders as he handed over the cheese and onion crisp box.

"There's a scrapbook about his mother's death, a manky teddy and a pregnancy test in there. We weren't certain whether it was positive or negative. Oh, and some floral notelets."

"You really should've called us earlier, sir."

"There didn't seem any point when no crime had been committed. We still don't know whether this Ignatius character has done anything wrong."

The police ignored his summing up of the situation.

"Your driving licence, sir?" one of the other officers interrupted.

Ian showed him the small card embedded with his photograph and he seemed satisfied.

"Is there anything else you want to tell us before we leave?"

The men were peering into corners and under the bed, as though they'd like to tear the place apart in search of clues. One officer was staring into the back garden.

"I think Ignatius tried to come back for his stuff the other day. I found a man fiddling with the lock. He pretended he'd got the wrong flat but when I saw the photo of him in the scrapbook I realised who he was."

"The lock was changed after he moved out of here?"

"Yes, the landlord had it done because Ignatius hadn't handed back his keys."

"As I said, sir," repeated the officer in charge, "you really should have told us all this earlier. You haven't done yourself any favours."

Then they left.

Ian realised he hadn't told them about last night's prowler. But they probably had enough to be getting on with for the time being. He sat on the bed and took deep breaths until he felt ready to tackle the rest of the day. The image of a hot shower hovered in his mind like a mirage. Pounding water, steam, the scent of citrus body wash and a huge thick towel: the craving to be clean was intense. He felt grubby and used. But the thought of the stained communal bath made his stomach heave. Instead, he had a thorough strip wash at the sink in his room followed by a mug of hot sweet tea and a huge bowl of Sugar Puffs.

When he felt human again, Marcus became Ian's priority. This morning should have been theirs to spend together and he wasn't going to let the opportunity slip away. He flicked through the hangers in his wardrobe for a clean shirt. He wanted different footwear, too; his trainers felt contaminated from his time at the police station. Ian groped in the darkness at the bottom of the wardrobe for his favourite casual shoes and pulled out the teddy bear.

Its glass eyes stared at him, expressionless. Whatever malevolence the furry bear had witnessed, it would never tell a soul.

He or Sandra must have pushed the teddy straight into the wardrobe rather than into the box when they'd tidied everything away the previous day. Now Ian would have to trail over to the police station with it and put himself under the spotlight again. But the bear would have to wait a few hours. Marcus came first this morning.

He didn't phone Josephine to warn her he was on his way over to collect his son. After her rude awakening, she'd invent some excuse to put him off. Ian wanted the advantage of surprise.

"I was hoping they'd locked you up," Josephine said when she opened the door. "I can't stop you living your vice-ridden life but I didn't think even you would stoop so low as to involve your own son."

"It was nothing like that and you know it. It was a simple case of mistaken identity."

"Whatever it was, it won't be happening to my son

again."

"I guarantee it won't happen again. Please may I come in or do you want all your neighbours to hear us rowing?"

Josephine stood aside and Ian stepped into the hall, removing his shoes without being asked.

"Where is he?"

"Gone swimming with a friend."

"Today was supposed to be my day!"

"When he turned up alone in a police car I thought you were indefinitely delayed."

Ian took a step closer to his ex-wife and put his hand gently on her arm. He felt her stiffen and she looked apprehensive but she didn't pull away.

"Josephine, we're both on the same side. We both want what's best for Marcus. Please can we be a bit more civil towards one another? We were in love once, remember?"

Josephine swallowed and nodded. "I'm doing my best to give him a proper upbringing without any bad influences." She emphasised the last two words and stared meaningfully at Ian. "So I want to be there next time you see him."

"That's not fair!" Ian's voice rose. Mothers had all the advantages when a marriage broke up.

"And it's not fair if you allow him to be corrupted by your seedy life."

She stepped away from him.

"I'll take you to court." Ian wanted to take back the words as soon as he'd said them.

"Do that. I can tell the court about the nightmares he has of the police breaking into his dad's home."

"They didn't break in and he doesn't have nightmares."

"He hasn't had chance yet. I'll text you a time and

place when you can next see him. I'll be chaperoning."

Ian drove home with clenched teeth. His tight grip on the steering wheel turned his knuckles white. Josephine had no right to treat him like this. Marcus was his son too. How stupid he'd been to think the three of them could ever be a family again.

Someone hissed his name as he reached the landing outside his bedsit in Vesey Villa.

"Ian!"

He looked around. The whisper was repeated.

"Ian!"

It was Sandra. She had her door open only a couple of inches. He stepped towards her and she reached out a hand, grabbed his jacket sleeve and pulled him into her bedsit. Halifax was sitting at the table crayoning.

"I didn't want you to walk in there unprepared. I had to warn you."

"What about?" asked Ian, automatically lowering his voice too.

Sandra looked pale and scared. His heart started to pound.

"I don't know if he's still in there."

"Who?"

"Ignatius. He was busting the lock on your door when I came back from the shops. He gave me a really evil look and I thought he was going to batter me with the hammer as well as your door lock." Sandra looked down at Ian's shoes. "I'm sorry about the police earlier. It was my fault. I didn't want to make things any worse for you than they already are so I haven't told the police about Ignatius breaking in just now."

Sandra looked close to tears and her words came out in a rush.

"It's O.K.," he said gently. "You had the best intentions."

118

"I'm sorry but I kept thinking about poor Maxine and what might have happened to her. I hardly knew her but she wasn't much older than me and she was always so kind to Halifax."

Ian looked at Sandra's despondent face.

"Don't worry."

"I think he's gone now. It's been quiet in there for about ten minutes. But I didn't want you to go charging in, just in case."

"You stay here and I'll take a look."

Despite Ian's request, Sandra followed him across the landing. The door to bedsit three was wide open and the lock was smashed. Inside it was obvious that someone had been searching. The wardrobe door was wide open and clothes were scattered over the floor. Cupboards had been rifled and stuff dropped everywhere as the intruder had failed to find what he wanted.

"The police took the box," said Ian. "Just the teddy bear was left behind. It was on the dining table when I went out."

"So Ignatius went away empty-handed?"

"Apart from the bear. Unless he had something else hidden that I hadn't found."

"Good." Sandra started picking shirts and trousers off the floor and putting them on hangers.

"I'll call a locksmith. I don't want to spend the night here without a proper lock on the door."

When most of the bedsit had been put to rights, Sandra made two mugs of tea. Ian retrieved the plastic box of Millionaire's Shortbread. There were only a few chunks left.

"I think we both need something sticky and sweet."

Ian took a large bite of his piece but Sandra nibbled delicately around the edge.

"It's a bit like eating a Cadbury's Crème Egg, isn't it?" Ian observed. "Everyone has a different way of doing it. I barge straight in, you savour it and Marcus makes it last too by eating it layer by layer, starting with the chocolate and ending with the biscuit. Here, take a piece for Halifax and let me know what she does with it."

Ian wrapped a piece of the confectionary in foil and handed it to Sandra. Their hands momentarily brushed together. He was startled by the spark that crossed from bare skin to bare skin. He looked at Sandra. She was looking at him, wide-eyed. He could tell she'd felt it too.

"I need to apologise about the other night," he said. "I was -"

"No need. I have to go now. I need to listen to Halifax do her reading book for school."

"Wait." Ian touched her hand and then couldn't think of anything to say to detain her. "Thanks for helping me tidy up."

"Thanks for the cake."

Sandra turned towards the door but made no move to leave.

"Could we share some wine again?"

It was a spur of the moment suggestion.

"I'd like that." She grinned. "I'm taking Halifax to Brownies later. They're having a pretend camping weekend in the church hall. She's been so excited, getting her sleeping bag and overnight stuff ready. So if you want to call round this evening, I'll be on my own."

Ian caught her gently by the shoulders and pulled her towards him. She offered no resistance. Her mouth was sweet from the shortbread. He let his arms drift down her back and she moved closer to him. He hadn't planned to kiss her or ask her out. But he was very glad he had. Sandra was soft, warm and responsive. After the constant recriminations from Josephine, Sandra restored his faith in womankind. She brought out his protective side in the way Josephine once had.

When she eventually pulled away her face was flushed.

"I really must get back to my daughter. She has instructions not to open the door to anyone but I don't like leaving her for too long."

"I'll see you later," he said.

As he swept up the mess around the broken lock, Ian pondered about Sandra. She was attractive, feisty, intelligent in a raw untutored sort of way, and principled. But the difference in their backgrounds was huge. And there was the age difference, too. Could they build any sort of future together? He couldn't imagine his mother approving of a young, purple-haired single mum. She'd jump to the same conclusion that Ian had on first meeting her. His mother would go out of her way to be pleasant to Sandra in the flesh. But as soon as she and Ian were alone, she wouldn't mince her words: "People like us are in a different social stratum and we don't mix with people like that."

Chapter Eleven

Teddy Bear was safe. The cheese and onion crisp box and its contents were lost but Teddy Bear was here. Ignatius held the worn, matted toy against his cheek and breathed deeply. His thumb went into his mouth and for a few minutes he found peace.

It was a long time since he'd been able to openly enjoy the comfort that Teddy Bear brought. The first time Maxine had seen him cuddling the bear she'd collapsed with laughter and assumed he was having her on. He'd realised then that seeking refuge in his childhood toy was outside the norms of society and he'd dropped Teddy Bear into the crisp box in the wardrobe. But sometimes, when Maxine was elsewhere, he'd sneaked him out again, curled up on the bed and sucked his thumb for half an hour. It made him forget that life and society didn't always welcome him with open arms.

Now, as he rubbed the matted fur against his skin, tension dropped from his shoulders and his thoughts stopped colliding with one another. He closed his eyes and dozed.

A white van was pulling on to the Vesey Villa forecourt when he awoke. Ignatius put Teddy down and became alert again. He'd been expecting the police. That silly girl from next door had given him poisonous looks as he broke the lock. She must have realised what he was doing. So he'd been as quick as possible inside the flat because blue lights could have arrived at any second. That's why he hadn't been able to find the cheese and onion crisp box, even though he'd completely emptied the wardrobe.

To get his hands on it he needed more time in the bedsit and a way of getting in that didn't draw attention. And there were still other things in the flat that could be useful. There was another tarpaulin in the dust on top of the wardrobe, which would be essential should Maxine's body need moving again. Heavy rain had been forecast and it might wash topsoil off the hillock and reveal her. If he dug her up, Maxine could be leaking body fluids, or he might need to chop her in half to fit her into a better final resting place. The yellow clinical waste sack was still in his mind. In each of these scenarios a second tarpaulin would be very useful for avoiding spillage.

His passport and driving licence were under the carpet near the fireplace. He didn't keep them there for secrecy, just so they didn't get lost. He'd need them to start a new life in a new place. It would be hard leaving Mother, but he wanted to live without watching his back all the time or dreading a newsreader announcing the discovery of Maxine's body.

The purple leaflet was still on the car dashboard in front of him. A resurrection would mean no dead body to worry about and Maxine could go away with him. Or they could stay here. He picked up the wrinkled paper and wondered if he should dial the number. Perhaps Maxine would get pregnant with another baby boy. This time he'd make sure she kept it.

The white van on the forecourt wasn't the police. There was an image of a key painted on its side. Ignatius gave Teddy Bear a final hug and placed him on the passenger seat of the car. He made his way over to the locksmith, who was getting tools out of the back of the van.

"Bedsit three?" Ignatius asked casually.

During his search of the bedsit he'd come across a letter with the new tenant's surname on it. He was about to use it to his advantage.

The locksmith nodded and looked questioningly at Ignatius.

"I'm the landlord," Ignatius said and offered his hand. "Mr Wolvestone told me he'd had a break-in. Sign of the times, isn't it? It's his responsibility to get the locks changed but as landlord I'm entitled to a spare key in case he absconds without paying his rent."

"Oh, yes." The locksmith was shutting the van and preparing to enter the building.

"Mr Wolvestone knows about it and I don't want him to have to pay for my key. Any chance I can pay you direct and take the key now? I'm in a bit of a hurry - I've a new tenant to show around another of my properties."

"Seems a reasonable request. Just let me clear it with Mr Wolvestone."

The locksmith disappeared into Vesey Villa. Ignatius waited outside. He could hear the locksmith call into bedsit three: "O.K. if your landlord has a spare key, Mr Wolvestone?"

"What? Oh yes, fine."

The locksmith reappeared at the front door and handed a small gold-coloured key to Ignatius.

"Just a fiver, mate."

Ignatius handed over the note, gave the man a

thumbs-up and then jogged down the road as if he were in a hurry. He didn't want to give the locksmith time to change his mind.

Now it should be easy to get his cardboard box of treasures back.

***

Sandra felt like a teenager with a date lined up. This morning's second glorious kiss had to be the precursor to magical things between her and Ian. He hadn't said what time he was coming. She looked at her watch again. The minute hand had hardly moved. It was just after ten past eight.

She checked herself in the mirror again. Her black skirt was just above the knee and hopefully wouldn't reveal too much thigh when she sat down. Her pink short-sleeved top was close-fitting but not so tight that it showed her nipples. Compared to most of the girls in this area she looked positively sophisticated. But did she look like a slut in Ian's world? She tried to imagine his ex-wife. It was difficult. Classy people didn't feature much in Sandra's life.

Perhaps if she had a job in Selfridges, Country Casuals, or even Marks and Spencer, she'd learn how the middle classes approached their clothes, makeup and appearance. Was it really all beige, brown and creams plus subtle scarves and the odd chunky piece of jewellery? It seemed like a uniform designed to make them blend into the background. Not really Sandra's cup of tea. Besides, she didn't have the money to renew Halifax's school uniform, never mind revamp her own wardrobe or get the hairdresser to tone down her hair until the purple grew out.

The heavy knock made her jump. She took a deep

breath. This was it: a proper date with a lovely man. Out of habit, she put the chain on the door before opening it a crack. A bottle of wine was brandished in the gap between door and frame.

"May I come in?" Ian's voice said.

Sandra removed the chain. For a moment they just stood and looked at each other.

He was wearing a pair of stone-washed blue jeans. It looked as though an inexpert man had tried to iron them. His shirt was checked in navy and sky blue. It had fewer creases than the jeans. Most people were better at ironing shirts than trousers because tops were washed more often than bottoms so they had more practice with them.

His feet were furry. It was grey, mouse-coloured fur. There were two eyes on each foot and some wonky whiskers that looked as if they'd seen better days.

"A Christmas present from Marcus," he said, following her gaze. "Josephine must have been feeling charitable. She let Marcus choose exactly what he wanted for me."

"Very nice." Sandra raised her eyes to his. "Halifax gave me a bag of chocolate buttons and a lolly."

"Sounds perfect."

"They were perfect. I can't give her pocket money, so she'd saved them from a friend's party bag for me and wrapped them in silver foil, which she folded to look like a Christmas cracker."

"Truly a case of it being the thought that counts."

"She's a darling. I don't know where I'd be without her."

Ian stepped further into the room and put the wine on the table.

"I could take you out if you … if you prefer. Have you eaten?"

"I had beans on toast a couple of hours ago."

"So, do you want to go out?"

"Where to?"

Sandra was groping for the right answer. Of course she wanted to be taken out by a man who was a cut above anybody she'd ever dated before. He'd treat her like a lady and she wanted to know how that would feel. But was it right to assume he'd pay for her? The money in her purse had to feed them for a week; she couldn't blow it all on one meal out. There might not even be enough for the sort of place that Ian was used to. And she didn't have the right sort of clothes ...

"I don't know the area yet. Where do you normally go?"

"I don't ... with Halifax, you know, going out is difficult." She felt awkward. She didn't want to say that no one with money had ever asked her out before. "The Golden Swan does lasagne and that sort of thing but it might not suit you."

"The pub across the road?"

She nodded.

"I collected my keys from there the first night. It didn't strike me as the most salubrious of places."

Now he was using words she didn't understand. She just nodded at him again. Whatever magic had been between them earlier was vanishing into the deep divide that separated their lives. How stupid of her to think there could ever be anything between her and a man who was closer in lifestyle to Kate Middleton than to single mum Sandra.

"Whatever," she said into the silence that hung between them. "This was a mistake, wasn't it?"

"What?"

"We don't have anything in common." There was no point in beating about the bush. "To you, eating out means crystal glasses, waiters in penguin suits and a menu in a funny language. I haven't eaten out at all this year. The last time was with a mobile car-washer, sent by one of my clients to collect her ironing when she couldn't come herself. I had sausage and mash washed down by one WKD in the Golden Swan and I paid for myself."

"Did you see him again?" asked Ian. "The car washer?"

"No."

"Good."

She raised her eyebrows wondering if he was jealous.

"I'd never let a lady pay for herself. If she's worth taking out she's worth paying for."

Sandra's heart fluttered; Ian was implying that she had some worth to him.

"Are you hungry?" she asked.

"A little. Why don't we compromise? Let's have a drink here and order a takeaway later? But next time, I promise, I'll treat you to a meal. I'll make some enquiries and get a restaurant recommendation. There's bound to be somewhere nice if we drive out of the city a bit."

'Next time'. The words bounced around her mind. Already he was planning a 'next time'. She'd talk a friend into having Halifax overnight. What could she wear? Nothing in her wardrobe would suit a swanky restaurant.

"Have you got a corkscrew?" Ian was pointing at the wine bottle.

"No."

"I'll be back in a minute. I'll fetch some glasses too."

Sandra's mind was still mentally flicking through her wardrobe when Ian came back. He set out the glasses and plunged the corkscrew into the bottle. This time the taste of the wine was familiar to Sandra and she didn't hanker after a Blue WKD.

"Where does Halifax sleep?" Ian asked, settling down on the settee and looking around the room.

Sandra pointed out the screen.

"The landlord took pity on me when Halifax grew out of her cot. He put that chipboard divider up to give the illusion of a bedroom. It's useless for keeping noise out but I have the TV volume very low and Halifax finds the murmur of voices comforting while she drops off to sleep."

"If I had plans to stay long term, I'd copy that idea for Marcus," Ian said. "Going to bed early last night on the settee was very frustrating."

Sandra tried to think of something interesting and witty to say to keep the conversation flowing. But her mind was blank. Someone like Ian was probably used to intelligent career women, not supermarket café waitresses.

"I'll put some music on."

She went quickly through her meagre CD collection and wondered if any of it was sophisticated. There was a classical CD in a cardboard sleeve emblazoned with 'Rachmaninov - Free with the Daily Mail!' It had probably never been played but it must have more class than some of her boy band stuff. Ian appeared to recognise it.

"Rachmaninov - you've got good taste."

He put his arm around her as she sat back down and she gently laid her head on his shoulder. Sandra knew this was where she wanted to be for the rest of life. She'd barely known the man a week but without doubt he was quality. Men like him didn't come along often.

A succession of bangs made them jump apart.

"What the …!" Ian twisted around to look at the

door.

There were more loud thumps on wood.

"I'll go."

Sandra put the chain on again.

"I'm looking for Maxine!" A high-pitched woman's voice screamed through the chained gap. "She lived at number three."

Before Sandra had chance to reply, Ian was leaning over her shoulder.

"It's me you want," he said. "I live at number three."

The woman let out a string of expletives.

"Getting angry won't help anyone. Let's try talking."

Sandra was amazed at the calmness in Ian's voice. He motioned her to release the chain. As she opened the door a young woman stumbled into the room and pounced on Ian, grabbing at his shirt.

"She didn't want kids and you got her pregnant! Where is she? She told me you were mental."

"No! You've got it wrong!" Sandra's voice rose to match the pitch and anger in the other girl's words. She wouldn't let Ian be wrongly accused and she pushed proprietarily in front of him. "This is the wrong man!"

"Ladies, please." Ian tried to step between them.

"She was in love with you but you let her down! You wouldn't support her. She had to go through the abortion alone. She's my friend and she'd never willingly have gone back to you!" The staccato sentences issued from the girl's mouth like bullets and made no sense. "Then those silly cards came in the post. It was obvious she didn't write them. She can write better than that and my surname wasn't even on the envelope - because you don't know it, do you? What have you done with her? And those texts don't fool no-one... "

The words 'double negative' went through Sandra's

130

mind and she looked at Ian. His face was a mixture of shell-shock and concern. The grammatical slip had passed him by.

"I got another one this morning telling me she'd found the perfect flat with you. How could that be true when you're still here?"

The girl paused in her diatribe, stepped closer to Ian and stared at him eyeball to eyeball. They were exactly the same height. Sandra could tell from Ian's expression that he didn't like this invasion of his personal space. But he didn't step away.

"I'm not Ignatius," he said slowly, his eyes fixed on the girl. "My name is Ian Wolvestone and I moved into bedsit three after Ignatius and Maxine moved out."

The girl's eyes darted between Ian and Sandra as if she were weighing up whether she was hearing the truth.

"So where are they, then?" Standing with clenched fists she looked ready to punch someone. "What's the forwarding address? People don't just disappear unless there's something funny going on."

"We don't know and it's nothing to do with us," said Sandra. "Now please leave my flat."

This unstable woman was ruining Sandra's romantic chances. All her dreams of escaping to a better life with this knight in shining armour were dissolving. Sandra did care about what had happened to Maxine, but for the next couple of hours Ian was the only person she wanted in her flat. Maxine could wait until the morning.

"No, don't go, sit down." Ian contradicted Sandra. "We can talk about this. Would you like a glass of wine? It might calm you a little."

Why was he being so bloody nice to the woman? This was supposed to be their time together and now it was spoiled. Sandra wanted to cry. She walked over to the window and looked into the blackness outside. Let them talk if they wanted to. She got precious few evenings to enjoy herself and this one had been ruined. If Ian really wanted to spend time with her, he'd have sent this mad woman packing. He was using this incoherent girl as an excuse not to be alone with her. She closed the curtains, turned around and watched them. Ian had fetched a tumbler from the draining board and half-filled it with wine.

The girl gulped at it as if it was the only water left in the desert. Even Sandra had more class than that. She wondered if the girl was an alcoholic. She looked the type.

"Put the kettle on, Sandra," Ian instructed as the girl pulled a tissue from up her sleeve and blew her nose. "The wine's good, but if we drink it at that rate all evening, we'll be under the table."

"Chance'd been a fine thing," Sandra muttered under her breath, wondering why she had suddenly become the skivvy and this other girl was sitting on the settee with Ian.

"There are chocolate biscuits in my flat. Go and fetch them." He threw her the key.

At least he hadn't asked for the Millionaire's Shortbread. Sandra didn't want to see Ian watching how sexily this impostor licked the toffee from between the chocolate and shortbread.

The two were sitting even closer together when she got back.

"What's your name?" Ian asked her. "This is Sandra, and as I've already told you, I'm Ian."

"Amy. Maxine's my best friend. I know her better than anybody and I know she wouldn't run off like this."

Sandra stood at the draining board with her back to

132

them, slowly stirring teabags and hot water in the mugs.

"The last time I saw Maxine she was in a right state," said Amy. She was calmer now and her voice had lost its aggression. She explained how Maxine had told her she was pregnant but terrified and believed she'd be a useless mother. "She told me she liked other people's kids but any child that had her as a mother would be better off never being born. Of course I told her that was rubbish and we'd all be here to help her with the baby. Then she said that Ignatius had started talking oddly when she'd told him about the baby. He said he only wanted a boy and he'd bring it up because mothers were a bad influence on boys. If it was a girl he wanted nothing to do with it. She said he was mental."

Amy paused and drank a mouthful of the tea that Sandra had placed in front of her.

"Not as good as the wine." She grinned and looked hopefully at the half-empty bottle. "Anyway, me and Maxine's mum could see Maxine was out of her mind with worry. So her mum helped her get the abortion. I think she was worried Maxine might top herself otherwise." She took a bite of chocolate biscuit and crumbs showered into her lap. "Then she rested for a couple of days before announcing she was finished with Ignatius and was coming round here to collect her stuff. She hardly had any clothes or things at her mum's by then - it was all in his bedsit. I offered to come with her but she wouldn't have it, she said she was a big girl now. It was something she wanted to do by herself."

Amy balanced the half-eaten biscuit on her knee and blew her nose again.

"We never saw her again after that. Of course we tried her mobile but she never picked up. But she did send some texts saying she and Ignatius were back together and starting a new life. Those put her mum's mind at rest but I felt something was wrong. The texts didn't sound as though Maxine had written them. When we received these notelets I was 99% sure something terrible had happened to her."

Amy handed two flowery cards to Ian.

"Don't touch!" Sandra said sharply.

They both looked at her.

"It's evidence, fingerprints and such."

She fetched a couple of flimsy sandwich bags and held them open whilst Amy dropped the cards in.

"Why don't you think they're from Maxine?" Ian asked.

"They don't say a lot," said Amy. "Just that they've moved to Derby and everything's going well. Ignatius has written them. He doesn't pretend otherwise. They've got a Derby postmark too, so at first I thought they might be genuine. But when I think about it, I can't see any reason for Maxine not to write the cards herself. So why did Ignatius do it for her? She must have been incapacitated."

"Have you been to the police?" Ian asked.

Amy nodded.

"They say we've no proof of foul play and all they can do is record her as missing. So we persuaded the newspaper to print that report."

"You should go again and demand action." As Amy's story took shape, Sandra forgot her animosity towards the young woman and remembered her previous concern for Maxine. "I went myself a couple of days ago and then they questioned Ian. But they seem to have done nothing since."

"Will you come with me to the police again?" Amy asked.

Sandra opened her mouth to speak but Ian got there first.

"It's a sad story about the baby," he said, "but the police will just say there's no new evidence of foul play. Maxine's made contact so I think you probably have to leave it at that. Sometimes people want to make a fresh start without the baggage of their old life. It's sad, but friendships do die or get outgrown."

Amy frowned and looked doubtful.

"But don't you think -" Sandra began.

"You haven't said anything to prove Maxine isn't safe and well in Derby," Ian interrupted. "I think that town should be your next stop. Get her picture into the paper in Derby and ask if anyone's seen her. I'm not being heartless, I'm just trying to pre-empt what the police will tell you. "

"Have you got a pen and paper?" Amy asked.

Sandra produced a piece of Halifax's drawing paper and a biro.

"That's my mobile number if you change your mind and want to help. But be warned - if Maxine doesn't turn up soon, I'll be back."

Then Amy left. The young woman's anguished tale had stolen the magic from the evening. It was half past nine and Sandra had imagined them in each other's arms by now. Instead, she was worrying about Maxine and Amy.

"I think we should have helped her," she ventured. "She knows Maxine a lot better than we do."

"Without evidence the police won't do anything." Ian seemed able to dismiss the whole affair as if the possible loss of a young girl's life was not important. "They've got the cardboard box and we've nothing else concrete to give them."

Sandra felt the special connection between them had loosened. Ian obviously sensed that things had shifted, too.

"I'll show myself out."

Chapter Twelve

It was warm in MacDonald's. The early morning Big Mac and hot sweet coffee were helping Ignatius thaw out after another night in the car.

When he'd finished his breakfast he'd use the facilities. His diet of cheap junk food was doing his insides no good. When Mum was alive she'd fed him prune juice or syrup of figs and her home cooking had included plenty of fruit and veg. He was always regular then. Even Maxine had cooked the odd green thing. Now his fibre intake was non-existent. When he did get the urge to go it was generally freezing cold and the middle of the night with no facilities around. It was O.K. weeing in the bushes but anything else he found abhorrent and fear of being spotted made him unable to relax and let go. Perhaps an orange juice and one of those hot apple pies might help.

The new bedsit key was safe in his pocket. He simply had to wait for the new tenant to go out and then he could slip in. This time he'd search the place methodically and not go at it like a madman again. A large cardboard box couldn't just disappear in a one-room flat.

But for now he'd content himself with contacting

Maxine's nearest and dearest once more and gently planting the idea in their heads that she was moving further away for a while. He didn't want suspicious cops poking around Vesey Villa until he'd recovered the box and made himself scarce. It was a shame he didn't have another notelet to send; posting it in Derby again would deflect any investigation well away from Vesey Villa and the body.

He pulled Maxine's phone out of his pocket. Texting wasn't his strong point and he didn't know most of the abbreviations that Maxine would probably have used. But he reckoned any sort of text would be gratefully received by her family and friends and would put their minds at rest.

"Been to travel agents. Planning a long holiday with Ignatius to get over the trauma of the past months. Will send you a postcard! Mxxxx"

He pressed send and the message went off to Maxine's mum.

Ignatius had never met her. He'd been invited several times but always made an excuse. He was wary of other people's mothers. He'd only met a handful and mostly as a schoolboy. Those visits had made him see that his mother was different, his own life was different, and that had upset him.

Sometimes Betty invited him in for a cup of tea when he took her shopping round. Now he always said no. But the one time he'd accepted she'd talked lovingly of her son in Australia, and Ignatius had suddenly realised the emotional poverty in which he'd grown up. He hadn't sensed any love from Mother. Sitting there in Betty's flat, his fists had clenched with anger and resentment.

Ignatius drained his coffee and headed to the Gents'.

Sandra had slept badly after the evening's events. Images of Ian flitted through her dreams. Sometimes he was with an imagined version of his posh wife, playing happy families. Then he was with Maxine's friend, Amy, at an expensive restaurant, offering her a diamond ring and a flowery notelet containing a love message that Sandra couldn't see well enough to read. In the final dream Sandra had been running. Ignatius was chasing her and brandishing a huge photograph in which her face had been obliterated. Ian was in front of her. She was trying to reach him. Her chest was bursting. Her legs were weak. Ian stared vacantly past her. She could hear Ignatius getting closer. Then she tripped. Fell. There was a sudden jolt and she was awake.

It was light outside. She'd slept later than usual.

Sandra put the kettle on and ate a bowl of Halifax's Sugar Puffs. She wondered if the Brownies were cooking breakfast in the church hall. She couldn't recall Halifax ever experiencing bacon, eggs and the full works first thing in the morning.

Then she remembered the takeaway that Ian had suggested for the previous evening and his offer to take her out for a proper meal 'next time'. Tears pricked behind her eyes. They'd parted on awkward terms. The business with Maxine and Amy had cooled things between them. So would there ever be a 'next time'? Was their disagreement her fault? She should've offered him some sort of olive branch.

Her mother had warned her that men needed treating with kid gloves. Sometimes, without meaning to, Sandra wore boxing gloves.

"Men like to feel in charge, Sandra," her mum had said many a time when her teenage daughter had complained about unsatisfactory males. "Everything has to be their idea. At least, they have to think it's their idea, even if you planted it in their heads to start with. It does nothing for their masculinity when they're told what to do by a woman."

But Sandra couldn't be bothered to pussy-foot around men and massage their egos. In her mind there was no point in calling a spade anything but a spade.

"That's why you never keep a man for long," her mum had said. "You intimidate them with your opinions and plans for how the two of you are going to be. It doesn't leave any room for what they want."

Sandra had taken no notice. She couldn't deny that her mother was well experienced with the opposite sex. Since she'd kicked Sandra's father out for playing away, there'd been plenty of male callers at their council flat. None had lasted more than a couple of months. So Sandra had little confidence in her mother's advice about men. But now she was willing to try anything to win Ian back.

He wasn't like the lads who hung around the flats with nothing to do, or the ones who contented themselves with earning the minimum wage by cleaning the supermarket where she worked. That sort would always be at the bottom of the class heap, happy as long as they had a council flat and money to drink on Friday and Saturday nights. Sandra wasn't happy with that. She wanted a go-getter, someone who'd make something of his life, someone who'd encourage Sandra to make something of her life; someone like Ian.

She wanted to ask him what he thought about her plan to go to college and get some qualifications. He'd know the best subjects to concentrate on. She imagined him helping with her homework and then explaining about job applications and CVs. The prospect of returning to the classroom wouldn't be so daunting with Ian backing her up.

Ian had had a 'proper' job and was looking for another. He'd owned a house and when he had a new job he'd own another. His upbringing had given him an advantage over the council-flat layabouts, but he must have worked hard at school and university otherwise he'd surely have fallen by the wayside. And, on a simpler level, he was a nice man and a good father who put his son first.

Plus, he was a great kisser. She closed her eyes and smiled as she remembered the touch of his lips, the taste of his mouth and the tenderness of his tongue. On the two occasions they'd kissed she'd felt closer to him than she ever had to any other male, including Halifax's father.

She wasn't going to risk losing Ian.

Sandra scrolled for Donna's number in her mobile. Donna was her best mate. But right now the most important thing about Donna was that she'd spent three months at hair-dressing college before having a baby forced her to abandon her career ambitions.

"Can you come over? And bring some blonde hair dye. I'll give you the money for it. And could you get a Sunday newspaper, one of those huge intelligent ones with a glossy magazine?"

Whilst she waited for her friend, Sandra dressed in her scruffiest jeans and T-shirt.

"Can you trim it or do something to make it less spiky?"

Sandra was sitting on a dining chair and Donna stood behind her, combing through the purple hair.

"Cutting will only make it spikier. You'll to have to let it grow, Sand."

"OK. Let's just do the colour then. Gentlemen prefer

blondes, don't they? Ian's a real gentleman."

The pair locked themselves in the communal bathroom with the packet of hair dye. Sandra had never changed her looks to please a man before. Like all women, she'd done herself up before a night out, but only to make the most of who she was. Everything had been her choice: hairstyle, makeup and clothes. But today she'd decided that Ian would probably take more kindly to a standard blonde than a purple-top who'd show him up in the posh places he frequented.

Once the messy bit was done they went back into Sandra's bedsit. Sandra's hair was still wet and she had her oldest towel around her shoulders.

"This isn't looking right." She peered into the tiny mirror in her room and touched her hair. "Does it look blonde to you? You did pick the right packet, didn't you?"

Donna waved the empty carton in front of her.

"Check it yourself. Let me dry it for you. Then it'll look better."

Sandra sat back on the dining chair whilst Donna brushed and blow-dried.

"Remember, no spikes."

Sandra closed her eyes while her friend worked. When she opened them she wanted to get the full impact of her new look, just as Ian would see it for the first time.

The buzz of the hairdryer ceased. Sandra was aware of a damp spray around her head and Donna's hand fiddling and gently stroking.

"I'm done," her friend said, "but it might not be quite what you wanted."

Sandra opened her eyes. She couldn't speak. Her reflection was horrific.

"My God, what have you done, Donna? It's ginger!"

"At least ginger's more natural than purple," Donna said quietly. "So you're going in the right direction."

"You are joking? I can't go out looking like this! Why hasn't it gone blonde? The packet said 'Ash Blonde'."

"I chucked in the hairdressing course before we did colouring. But I think maybe it's because your hair was such a strong purple to start with. Perhaps it needed bleaching first."

"So what do I do now?"

"I could come back and bleach it tomorrow, if Mum will look after Wayne again for me."

Donna looked as upset as Sandra felt.

"No! You're not touching my hair ever again."

"I'll leave you my scarf. It would look quite classy wrapped around your hair." Donna seemed close to tears. "I'm sorry. This has never happened to me before. I won't take your money for the dye. Use it to buy another scarf; they're quite cheap in the market."

Donna left, full of apologies. Sandra flung the scarf over the mirror so that she couldn't see herself. Then she burst into tears. She didn't have enough money to have her hair put right professionally. She'd have to live with it until it grew out.

But Ian mustn't see her like this. Not only was her hair a horrible shade of ginger but the texture had gone like wire. It was not the sort of thing a classy man would want to run his fingers through. Ian was used to women with expensive, regular haircuts.

She gazed down at The Sunday Times that Donna had dropped on the settee. She'd hoped to gather intelligent subjects to talk to Ian about. But what was the point of reading the paper when she'd never have the chance to converse with Ian anyway?

***

143

Ian stood outside the tea room in the Museum and Art Gallery. This was Josephine's choice of somewhere neutral for her and Marcus to meet him.

He'd phoned her at nine o'clock that morning, as early as he'd dared on a Sunday.

"Can we meet this afternoon?" he'd suggested. "You know, the chaperoned visits you were talking about?"

"It's a bit soon, isn't it? You only saw him yesterday morning."

"I didn't exactly see him. We both got carted off separately by the police, if you remember? Besides, if I don't see him today, you'll make me wait until next weekend because of school, your work, homework, after school activities... There's a 101 possible excuses you can use midweek, so let's do it now."

There was a long pause before Josephine replied.

"In the absence of anything better to do, Marcus and I will meet you. What about afternoon tea in the Museum?"

"Sounds very civilised. Will Marcus be all right with that?"

"Yes. He could do with some culture."

Now Marcus and Josephine were walking down the museum gallery towards him. They were ten minutes late.

"We were looking at some of the beautiful paintings as we came in. I didn't realise the time otherwise I'd have hurried him along. Fascinating, wasn't it, Marcus?"

Marcus nodded his head without enthusiasm.

"Are we going to have cakes now, Dad?"

"Perhaps just a small one," Josephine said cautiously and threw a look at Ian that said 'Do not encourage him to have a big unhealthy cream cake'.

Ian found it odd that as their marriage disintegrated his wife had often declared they had 'communication

144

problems', but now they were divorced she managed to say such a lot without words.

"Let's go in," he said.

They went through the archway from the gallery into the large, high-ceilinged tearoom. It was alive with chatter and there was an enticing smell of hot food. Weak October sunshine came in through glass panels overhead and the oil paintings around the walls added to the special atmosphere. Ian thought what a great treat it would be to bring Sandra and Halifax here. Having so little, they'd really appreciate it.

He picked up a brown wood-effect tray. It still held a small pool of water from an over-zealous tray-cleaner.

"Why don't you tell me what you want to eat, Josephine, and then you can grab us a table whilst Marcus and I stand in the queue?"

"No, I'll stick with you."

He sighed. She was intent on taking this self-imposed chaperoning business to the nth degree - or she didn't trust him not to allow Marcus to have the biggest, most unhealthy cake and cream concoction on offer.

"A pot of tea, please," she said to the uniformed girl behind the counter.

"What about something to eat?"

Ian gestured at the glass-fronted cabinet in front of them.

Josephine patted her flat stomach. "Nothing, thanks."

Marcus asked for a coke and then pointed at a large chocolate éclair oozing cream.

"I don't think …" began Josephine.

"Make that two chocolate éclairs," Ian interrupted. "I fancy one too. And I'll have a large latte."

This time together in the café promised to be awkward enough without them all sitting there wishing they'd had something nicer to eat or drink. Sandra's purple head popped into his mind again. She'd have no problem selecting a nice cake and allowing Halifax a treat. He decided to take the two of them out the next weekend, along with Marcus. Josephine couldn't keep up this silly chaperoning.

"Sorry about that business with the police yesterday," he said to Marcus as they settled themselves at a table. "It was a case of mistaken identity. I hope it didn't upset you?"

"It was great, Dad. I've never been in a police car before. They wouldn't let me have the siren on but I did get a go with the blue lights."

"Sounds exciting," said Ian and gave his son's foot a gentle kick under the table. "As long as you're not a criminal."

Josephine stirred her tea and stared silently at it. Marcus ate the chocolate éclair much as he ate Millionaire's Shortbread. He licked the chocolate icing off the top first and then used his tongue to capture as much of the fresh cream as possible before finally biting into the choux pastry.

"Please can you eat it normally?" Josephine asked.

"But Dad lets me …"

Ian shook his head and put his fingers to his lips to silence his son. There was no point antagonising Josephine further.

When they'd all finished eating and drinking, Josephine said "Shall we have a walk around the exhibits now?" Her voice was too bright.

"Is the dinosaur still here?" Marcus stood up. "We saw it before once."

He trotted in front of his parents looking for the dinosaur gallery.

"So can I have him on my own again now you've

vetted me?"

"That bedsit place of yours isn't suitable. Not after yesterday."

"How about I collect him from your house, take him out for a couple of hours and then bring him back?"

"How do I know you're not going to take him back there?"

Then Marcus raced back to them and put an end to the conversation. They both joined in the boy's excitement at the large model of the tyrannosaurus rex. Josephine started smiling and seemed to relax. Ian stood by its head and made the noises he thought the giant creature might have uttered when it roamed the earth. Marcus and Josephine both fell about laughing just as a security guard walked past and gave them all an odd look. Ian didn't care about the guard; it was good to feel part of a family again and wonderful to see Josephine enjoying herself in his company. He roared even louder. Then Marcus grabbed both his parents' hands and the threesome walked along joined in a line.

"Look, Marcus! Paper and crayons." Josephine pointed with her free hand to a small table in the middle of the next gallery. It was laid out with children's drawing equipment. "Can you do us a masterpiece like those on the wall?"

"Good idea," said Ian. "You've got some great pictures on the wall at school."

Marcus removed his hands from his parents' and joined their hands together before running over to the table. Ian felt the tension flow between him and his ex-wife as they stood together beside the drawing table. He expected her to let go and feign interest in one of the pictures on the wall. But she stayed joined to him. He glanced sideways at her just as she was looking at him. They shared a half-hopeful, half-questioning expression.

Then Marcus came back to them waving a piece of paper. Josephine loosed their hands so she could take it from him. Ian felt that a wobbly rope bridge had been built.

Chapter Thirteen

There was a knock at the door. Sandra's heart leapt. Few people called at the bedsit without warning. Ian was the only recent one.

She glanced around the room to make sure it looked tidy. Halifax, exhausted from her overnight antics with the Brownies, was sitting at the dining table colouring. The bed was made and the sink wasn't full of unwashed pots. The room was presentable for Ian.

Then, like a punch in the stomach, Sandra remembered her hair. She'd hidden it under Donna's scarf when she went to collect her daughter but there'd been a gasp of shock when she'd revealed herself at home.

"Mum! You look so … different," her daughter had said diplomatically.

"Can I go out looking like this? Or should I keep wearing the scarf?"

"It's a shock at first but people will get used to it."

The knock sounded again. Sandra didn't want to give Ian the same shock that Halifax had had. She quickly wound the scarf around her head and opened the door. Amy was halfway into the flat before Sandra realised she'd forgotten to use the chain.

"You have to help me!" Amy was in a panic, gibbering. "Something terrible has happened to Maxine and he's trying to throw us off the scent. He wants to stop us searching for the body until the trail's gone cold, and then it'll be too late to do anything!"

"Mum?" Halifax had abandoned her colouring and was looking nervously from the stranger to her mother.

"Sit down, Amy. I'll make us a drink. It's all right, Halifax. Amy is a friend of Mummy's and has come round to say hello."

Amy appeared to notice Halifax for the first time. She gave the little girl a weak smile.

"Will you come to the police with me?" Amy asked when the two women were settled with mugs of hot tea.

Sandra inclined her head towards Halifax and put her finger to her lips. Then she switched the television on to distract her daughter from the adults' conversation.

"You said they weren't interested last time you went. They just put her down as a missing person."

"I've had another text today and so has her mother. It said they're going on holiday, Maxine and Ignatius."

"That's good. Maybe they're back together again big time." If all appeared to be well, why was Amy panicking? "So you're going to tell the police she's O.K.?"

"No! The text doesn't sound like her. It's the sort of text my great-grandma would send, long-winded and without the abbreviations everyone uses. Maxine didn't write the text. Someone less mobile-savvy did."

"It came from her phone, though?"

"Yes. He could easily have kept her phone and sent these messages to make it look like she was still alive. Ignatius never had a mobile at all until he started seeing Maxine. She had to force him to buy one. And then she

150

had to teach him to use it. When they were living here, he texted me once to say Maxine was ill and couldn't meet me at our usual time. He wrote it like it was a letter to school, all correct grammar and stuff. He even used commas."

"Are you sure it couldn't have been Maxine?"

Amy nodded. "Positive."

Sandra couldn't bear the thought of Maxine having been killed or hurt and no one bothering to help her.

"This is new evidence," Amy persisted. "If you come and back me up with what you know about that murdering sod Ignatius, they'll be much more likely to believe me."

"But I don't know anything concrete. I don't know if he's hurt Maxine."

Amy stood up and stamped her foot.

"Just because that middle-class twat says the police won't want to know, that doesn't mean it's true."

Out of the corner of her eye, Sandra could see Halifax glancing anxiously at them.

"You don't have to agree with him," Amy continued. "He's not the police."

Sandra couldn't stop the colour rising in her cheeks.

"You fancy him, don't you?" said Amy

Sandra nodded.

"He's the nicest man I've ever met. I've already screwed up once with him and the police. I don't want to do it again."

Amy appeared to contemplate this and then she spoke slowly.

"If you come with me, you'll have the chance to paint Ian in a good light. You can ask the police to tread carefully where he and his bedsit are concerned. But if I go alone and persuade them to take action they'll go barging straight in there. Plus, your middle-class man might remain forever out of your reach anyway, in which case you'll have let Maxine down for no reason."

Amy's last sentence made Sandra's mind up. Once Ian saw her ruined hair, and coupled it with yesterday's police visit and her social inferiority and all the other things that meant they weren't a good match, there'd be little chance of any love affair.

"O.K. I'll come with you. But let me get Halifax to bed first and I'll call my friend to babysit."

Donna could pay her back for the hair fiasco.

It was the same young policeman on the desk. He examined the texts on Amy's phone and made some notes.

"These texts don't mean the sender has done anything violent," he said, looking up. "But I'll record your concerns."

Amy looked as though she was about to throw a tantrum in the main lobby of the police station. Sandra put a hand on her shoulder.

"You've done your best, Amy. When the police review everything we've said as a whole, it might make more sense to them."

She glanced at the policeman behind the desk. He shook his head and sighed.

***

Ian relaxed on the settee and put his arm across Marcus's shoulders. Uncharacteristically, the boy moved in closer for a cuddle. Josephine placed a mug of tea for him on the coffee table. Buster stirred in his sleep in front of the gas fire. Everything was as it should be in a family.

"He's dreaming about chasing rabbits," explained

152

Marcus, reaching his leg out to stroke the dog with his foot. "And he's really happy now he's allowed in the house."

"I'm going to have nice dreams tonight, too," said Ian. "We've all had such a lovely afternoon together."

"I wish you didn't have to go, Dad."

"Me too."

Ian glanced across at Josephine who was settling herself on the settee at the other side of Marcus. She frowned, shook her head and mouthed the words, 'not yet'. Ian sighed.

"But when I've finished this tea, I'll have to go, son. You've got school in the morning, Mum's got to go to work and I must find myself a new job."

***

Next morning, Ian was at his laptop early. This new job was taking too long to materialise. The sooner he was gainfully employed, the sooner Josephine might consider reconciliation.

His mobile rang.

"It's James Hudson from Copper Plate Computing. We may have an opening for you."

James explained that although Ian wasn't the best candidate for the job they'd advertised, they did have another vacancy. It would require two months' training in the company's Birmingham office followed by a year in Dubai leading a special project team. After that he'd be based permanently in Birmingham.

"So what do you think?" James asked. "Are you interested?"

"I …it's not what I expected." Ian's mood had gone from elation at the job offer to indecision when he learned what it entailed. "Can you give me time to think it over?"

"I can give you twenty-four hours. We need someone in post quickly."

Ian's mind raced as he put the phone down. Going to Dubai was likely to dash any chance of reconciliation with Josephine. After what happened in Amsterdam she wouldn't trust him to be away 'on business' for twelve months. And what about Marcus? Ian had moved to the Midlands to see more of his son. The boy would grow and change out of all recognition during the year Ian was away.

But being unemployed wasn't cementing his fractured family together, either. This new role was well paid and when he came back there'd be a job here waiting for him. The extra money could be invested as a nest egg for Marcus. It would give him a great start when he grew up and wanted to buy a house or a car.

Ian needed to talk this over with someone, someone who could be objective about his financial and emotional situation, someone sensible and down to earth.

Sandra. She was the only person in this city he could approach. Josephine came with too much baggage from the past. But first he'd have to clear the elephant from the room after what had happened, or rather not happened, between him and his neighbour the other evening.

Given how well Sunday had turned out with Josephine and Marcus, Amy's arrival on Saturday night had been a blessing in disguise. It had stopped things developing any further between him and Sandra. But there was a definite connection between the two of them and he wanted to keep her as a friend. He hoped she'd understand and accept that.

There was a longer pause than usual after he knocked

on Sandra's door before she put the chain on and opened it.

"It's only me," he said when she eventually peered out. "Can we talk?"

"Well, I ..." She seemed reluctant to open the door.

Did she have someone else in the flat with her? A man? None of his business if she did, he told himself.

"If you're busy ..."

He turned to go back across the landing.

"No, come in."

She was wearing a purple headscarf. It seemed hastily tied. A scrap of ginger hair had escaped from it and lay on her forehead. There was more around the neckline. Her fingers were busy trying to push the locks back inside the scarf as she let him into the flat.

"Have you changed the colour of your hair?" he asked.

For a moment her face seemed about to crumple into tears, but then she regained her composure.

"Just an experiment with a friend who knows a bit of hairdressing. You know what girls are like. Do you want tea?"

"No, thanks. But I would like to see your hair."

He'd hated the purple to start with but then he'd realised it was part of who Sandra was. He wanted to know what this feisty young woman had chosen to do with her hair now.

"My hair's not important. What did you come round for?"

Her voice was edgy. Something wasn't right. Women were always keen to show off a new hairdo and fish for compliments.

"I wanted your opinion."

"My opinion?" She sounded shocked. "I'm not qualified to give an opinion on anything."

155

Ian noticed yesterday's Sunday Times open on the dining table. This girl never ceased to amaze him. He couldn't believe he'd dismissed her on first meeting as not worth bothering with.

He told her about the job.

"So you won't be able to pop home for the weekend to see Marcus? After twelve months your relationship with him will be worse than before you moved here. Not good, I'd say."

"But the money is excellent, so there'll be a nest egg for when he's older. And being unemployed isn't helping anything."

"You said your father was good financially but you missed his emotional input."

Ian nodded.

"But this secondment isn't forever and it's a great learning opportunity. I'll be working with cutting edge technology, which will be great for my CV."

"I don't want you to go." Sandra's cheeks coloured and she stared at the floor. "And I'm sure Marcus would prefer you here."

Ian took a deep breath. He hadn't realised the depth of Sandra's feelings for him. Now he was about to hurt her even more.

"There's another complication. I'm hopeful that Josephine and I might get back together."

Sandra looked up. Her mouth had twisted and her eyes were wide with anguish. Ian's heart tightened. They were both silent for a while. She blew her nose. He put a hand on her shoulder, meaning to comfort her; but she stepped away, shrugging him off. When she spoke again there was a slight shake to her voice.

"I went to the police with Amy last night. I had to."

"Why? There's no new evidence."

"Amy got a text supposedly from Maxine but written

156

in old person's text speak. She knew Ignatius had written it and I believed her. If I hadn't gone I couldn't have lived with myself. No doubt the police will be back here when they've got their act together. Probably getting back with … Josephine is the … best thing. You'll be away from … all this mess."

Sandra's last words were mumbled. Then she lost control and sobbed.

Ian stared at her hunched figure. He wanted to hold her close. He wanted to kiss her and make everything better again. In fact he very much wanted to kiss her. But that was out of the question.

She looked up with red teary eyes.

"Whatever you do about the job you'll have to move," she said. "Josephine will never let Marcus near Vesey Villa again with all this weird stuff going on."

Then she cried harder. With a lump in his throat, Ian walked towards the door. By staying here he was only prolonging the agony for them both.

"Don't let anyone ever put you down," he said. "You're one of the best."

"That's it, isn't? The end of us, before it even began."

He nodded slowly.

"No point trying to impress you any more, then."

She pulled the purple scarf from her head, and while he was taking in her new garish ginger locks she picked up The Times and dumped it in the bin.

"What?"

"I was trying to make myself more classy and intelligent. Gentlemen prefer blondes so I tried to dye my hair and I wanted to discuss current affairs with you. I wanted you to introduce me to your friends without being embarrassed by my social status. Or lack of social status."

He was bowled over by the effort she'd made.

"Sandra, I don't know what to say."

"Don't say anything. The hair looks crap and I was stupid to think that I could ever be anything but … stupid."

"I agree the hair colour isn't great. The purple was better. I was even getting quite fond of the shade. But your brain is fine, brilliant. Go to college, make something of yourself."

"Just leave."

She started to cry again.

Chapter Fourteen

Ian scrolled through his contacts. The next step was to phone Josephine and discuss what the Copper Plate Computing job might mean for their situation and Marcus. Would she, like Sandra, prefer him to stay?

"Ian, I'm at work. Can we talk some other time?"

"Meet me for lunch, please? I've had a job offer but it means twelve months in Dubai. I have to discuss it with you today. There's a coffee shop around the corner from your office. I'll be there at one o'clock."

Ian paced around the bedsit, his brain hopping between the job, Sandra, Josephine and Marcus. He stared out of the window. The rain was continuing to affect the hillock of soil. Much of it had been washed down on to the lawn and the heap appeared to be sinking in the middle.

He looked at the wall between his flat and Sandra's. He regretted those kisses, regretted giving her false hope that they could have had a future together. Was she still crying? Some women turned on the waterworks at the drop of a hat, but Sandra's tears were genuine. She couldn't pull the wool over anyone's eyes. She was one in a million. Was he stupid for walking away from her and back into a marriage that had failed once already?

He arrived much too early at the coffee shop and had already drunk one cappuccino when Josephine arrived.

"I haven't got long," she said, nodding at the waitress.

She ordered a skinny decaf latte and a humus sandwich. Ian asked for another cappuccino; he had too much on his mind to eat. Whilst his ex-wife ate, Ian explained about the job offer from Copper Plate Computing and its implications. She put the sandwich down.

"So you'll have plenty of chance to pick up where you left off in Amsterdam."

"That was a stupid one-off incident on my part and you know it."

"It's none of my business now anyway. We're divorced, remember?" Her voice was higher than usual. "And you're right; the year away will help save some money for Marcus's future. He'll be upset that you're leaving just as he was getting used to you again, but kids are adaptable. Take the job if you want it."

Josephine clasped her hands tightly together and rested them on the table. From experience, Ian could tell she was upset but trying to act like she didn't care. He couldn't gauge whether she meant what she said about being happy for him to go away or whether she was hiding her true feelings, and thus her vulnerability, from him.

"Is that really what you want? What would it do to us?"

"There is no 'us'."

"But yesterday was great. I thought things were improving between us and with me being here, close by, we could perhaps …"

"Yes, we all enjoyed yesterday, but Amsterdam still

happened, didn't it? At the moment I really don't know whether we could be together as a couple again. So the decision about the job has to be yours, Ian. Don't pass the buck to me."

Josephine picked up her handbag and walked out of the café.

***

Ignatius stared at the tail end of his evening pint in The Golden Swan. Today was not going well and the constant rain against the pub window meant it would get worse.

He'd seen the new tenant of bedsit three go out at lunchtime and had seized the opportunity to use his key from the locksmith. His passport and driving licence had been where he'd expected, beneath the carpet. Then he searched for the cardboard box. He knew from his previous visit that it wasn't in the wardrobe but desperation made him check again. He'd found no trace of it.

Despite his frustration, Ignatius had tidied carefully after his search. He couldn't afford to arouse suspicions about a break-in. He'd too much to lose if the police appeared and started nosing around.

Before he left he'd glanced out of the bedsit window. What he saw frightened him. The wet weather was taking its toll on the earth covering Maxine's grave. Some of the soil had been washed away and the rest appeared to be subsiding. It might be to do with the resurrection, the dead being able to live again. It was becoming easier for Maxine to break out of the grave.

All afternoon he'd been listening to the weather forecasts and watching the puddles grow in the tarmac around the car. Warnings of severe weather and floods had been given. It was only a matter of time before the rest of the earth sank deeper into the grave or washed off completely. He had to move her body tonight, before it was discovered.

The yellow clinical waste bag still seemed a good idea. Once that was taken away and incinerated he'd have nothing to worry about. But Maxine would have to be dismembered to fit into it and Ignatius didn't have a saw.

"You should have planned ahead," his mother whispered in his ear. "How do you think I held down three cleaning jobs, did my own housework and had a hot dinner on the table for you every evening?"

Ignatius shook his head to dislodge the whining voice. It wouldn't budge.

"He who doesn't think ahead is lost," she continued.

Ignatius took deep breaths and tried to marshal his thoughts. Even if he'd had a saw, he told himself, the yellow sack was a bad idea. It might incriminate Betty and that was the last thing he wanted to do to the old lady. At the very least she'd be scared out of her mind.

The river was the best option for dumping Maxine. She'd be washed ashore in a short time but it would be away from Vesey Villa and the police would find it difficult to pin anything on him. Maxine could've been murdered anywhere along the bank and then dropped in. There was no reason for them to think he was connected to her death. Anyway, he intended to be as far away as possible when the body was discovered.

Ignatius knew from the television that water did horrible things to dead bodies. It would probably remove trace evidence, fingerprints, fibres and anything else that could tie him to the crime.

He ordered another pint and managed to make it last until eleven o'clock, despite pointed looks from Maud behind the bar. He had to go easy on the drink; there was no point trying to move Maxine whilst he was pissed. It would be hard enough sober. And he couldn't risk being stopped and breathalysed by the police.

"See, Mother. I am planning ahead," he whispered to himself.

The rain soaked him through on the short walk from the pub doorway to his car. As soon as he was inside the Volvo the windows steamed up. He turned the key to start the engine and demist the windscreen. The engine puttered twice, and then nothing. He tried the ignition again and then again. Nothing. Ignatius thumped the steering wheel and cursed when the horn blared.

One more turn of the key, he told himself, one more turn of the key and the damn thing would spring into life. He took the key out of the ignition, put it back in, took a deep breath and crossed the fingers of his left hand whilst turning the key with his right. There was still no response. He swore.

Now how was he going to move Maxine? He'd planned to reverse the car on to the paved frontage of Vesey Villa, as near the side gate as he could get. Then there'd only be a short distance to manhandle her before he could dump her in the boot, and she'd be hidden from view. Without transport he couldn't get her to the river.

The drumming on the roof of the car was easing. Ignatius opened the door and stuck his arm out. The downpour had become drizzle. He might not have to move her tonight after all. In the morning he could get a new battery and the car problem would be solved. To be sure, he needed to check the state of her grave. As he approached the house, he saw the familiar red glow from the front window of the top bedsit, but Betty's flat was already in darkness.

Going down the side path he heard yowling and stiffened. Foxes. He didn't want their noise drawing attention to him.

He shut the side gate behind him and looked up at the back windows of Vesey Villa. One side was in darkness. The child that Maxine had been so fond of must be in bed, and so must its mother. There was still a light on in his old room. It cast some illumination on the back garden, which helped his inspection.

The fox was standing next to the sinking mound and letting rip with its voice every now and again. Ignatius ran at the animal, hoping to frighten it away, but it stood its ground and howled again. The end of the grave had sunk furthest. There was now a definite trough in the earth at this point, and something was lying on the ground in front of the animal.

Ignatius bent for a closer look and then staggered backwards. It was a hand. Despite the black loose skin, he was sure it was a hand. It was sticking up through the soil. Maxine was waving for help. This was her resurrection. She wanted him to take her hand and pull her up into the land of the living. He went nearer and reached out tentatively. But millimetres before their skin made contact he recoiled. He couldn't do it. He stamped on the hand. He stamped on it hard, again and again and again. It cracked and crunched beneath his feet. The fox scarpered to the other end of the garden. Ignatius kept raising his foot and then bringing it down with all his strength.

The purple leaflet had told him about the dead living again and he'd been pleased. But if Maxine came back to life she wouldn't be pleased with him. She'd remember the tight grip of his hands on her neck and the slow squeezing until her breath was all gone. And he couldn't forgive what she'd done to their baby son. She didn't deserve resurrection. Ignatius would have to kill her all over again.

He kicked the hand. It was discoloured and lifeless and remained stuck in the same patch of earth, attached to a buried arm. Cautiously, Ignatius kneeled down and pawed at the soil with bare hands. He tried not to breathe in the stench or touch the limb. Eventually he could see more of the arm. Its condition reassured him that no resurrection was possible. During her time underground, Maxine had suffered the ravages of nature.

Ignatius relaxed slightly but he still had a problem. The whole body needed reburying more deeply. Or he had to move her. Something had to be done tonight before the fox or the rain revealed more.

He tried to think logically. There were pros and cons to each course of action, but with that hand and its chipped red nail varnish taunting him, it was impossible to make a sensible decision.

"Take deep breaths," whispered his mother, "and gather your thoughts."

He grabbed handfuls of earth from beneath the rose and roughly covered the exposed flesh. The fox crept closer and started its chorus again. This time it didn't stop with a couple of yowls. It went on and on and on. Ignatius put his hands over his ears.

Suddenly the animal was bathed in light. Then the light went off again. Ignatius looked up and saw the resident of bedsit three looking down. He'd been seen. His decision had been made for him.

***

The noise of the fox had brought Ian to the window

but he sensed the animal wasn't alone. He turned out the light and waited for his vision to adjust to the darkness outside. Someone was in the garden by the sinking pile of soil. As Ian looked down, the man looked up. It was difficult to make him out in the blackness but Ian had no doubt who it was. Ignatius had come back again.

He went over to the party wall and listened for any sign that the fox had disturbed Sandra. There was nothing.

He picked up his mobile to call the police. Then the sound of a key turning in his own door lock made him pause. He put the phone down slowly. No one had a spare key except the landlord, who'd taken one from the locksmith.

The door opened and light from the landing flooded the dark room. Ian stood like a rabbit in headlights. The intruder was a silhouette. A hand lifted the large serrated vegetable knife from the draining board and brandished it like a knight going into battle.

Ian backed against the wall. The man flicked on the room light. And then Ignatius moved slowly towards him. As he got closer, Ian could see the threat in his eyes. The blade rose and touched the underside of Ian's chin. He could smell the sour breath of his assailant.

"There's a job I need some help with."

Ian didn't speak. He was trapped in a corner now. There was nowhere to go.

"And you are going to be my aide. There's a tarpaulin on top of the wardrobe. Get it down."

Followed by the blade of the knife, Ian dragged a dining chair over to the wardrobe. He stood on it and felt in the dust on top of the ancient double wardrobe.

"I can't …"

The knife nicked his leg through his jeans. Ian leant

further over and reached his hands to the back of the wardrobe. If he slipped, the knife would slice into his leg.

His fingers met something heavy but pliable. He pulled at it and the tarpaulin came over the raised carvings on the front of the wardrobe. Those decorative twirls had hidden it. For a split second he wondered if he could drop it on Ignatius and roll him up in it. But the chance was gone as the intruder reached up and took the tarpaulin from him.

"Into the garden."

Ignatius grabbed the upper part of Ian's arm as he stepped down from the chair. He held the knife to the side of his neck. They met no-one as they went down the stairs to the front door. Outside, the damp, cold air clung to Ian and he shivered in his shirt sleeves. He noticed Ignatius was dressed for the weather in a thick jacket. They went round the back. The fox had gone. Ignatius stood behind Ian, marching him to the shed. He made him retrieve a spade from inside the decrepit wooden building.

"Dig over there." Ignatius pointed to the earth mound.

"Why?"

The knife caught the skin on his left forearm where the sleeve was rolled up.

Ian started digging. The soil was heavy and wet. There was an unpleasant smell. After only a few spadesful he hit something that wasn't earth.

"Stop."

Ignatius shone a torch around the spot where Ian had been digging. It was the area where the hand had appeared above the soil. Ian saw it for the first time now and almost screamed. Then Ignatius moved the beam of light and illuminated what the shovel had hit.

The hair was tangled and matted. It was coming away from the head. The face was repulsive.

"God Almighty!"

Maxine. This had to be Maxine's body. Sandra had been right to go to the police. He staggered to his feet, looking for lights in neighbouring houses. He raised his arms, ready to wave and draw attention to his predicament. He opened his mouth to shout. The knife caught him on the neck. Ian felt the warm trickle of blood.

"We need to move her. Carry on digging. Carefully."

Ian continued. His shoulders started to ache, then his back. He wanted the toilet. He was frozen to the bone. Slowly, Maxine's body was appearing before him.

There was a second tarpaulin beneath her, which had obviously been meant to wrap the whole body. But it hadn't been secured properly.

"That's enough."

Exhausted, Ian let the spade fall to the floor and bent over to release the muscles in his back.

"We need to wrap her in the tarpaulins otherwise there'll be evidence all over your car."

"My car?"

"Do it."

Ignatius had to put the knife down and help with the operation. One man alone couldn't manhandle the repulsive body and arrange its wrappings.

Ian's brain worked fast. The side gate was the only exit. Ignatius was between him and the gate. But Ian had the more athletic build. He could do it. He dropped the tarpaulin and sprinted.

A second later there was a thump and then mud filled his eyes, mouth and nose. He'd gone flying into the grave just vacated by Maxine.

"Pull a stunt like that again and I'll do more than

stick my foot out to trip you."

After a few minutes the body was securely wrapped and fastened into the tarpaulins with a roll of heavy duty tape that Ignatius produced from his jacket pocket.

Chapter Fifteen

Sandra lay still and listened. She could hear voices. Did Ian have a visitor? It didn't sound like the television. She switched on the bedside light and looked at her watch. Just after midnight. For a split second she felt a pang of jealousy. Who might be in Ian's bedsit?

The words were indistinguishable but one voice grew louder. The speaker was a man giving orders and he sounded angry. Wide awake now, Sandra got out of bed and listened at the party wall. Nothing. The noises weren't coming from Ian's flat. She went to the window and moved the curtain a couple of centimetres. She was looking down on to the side path and two figures were moving along it. They were carrying something. A roll of carpet? She couldn't see properly. They laid whatever it was in the side passage. Sandra eased the window open, hoping to hear more clearly.

"... car keys." The first words of the sentence were lost to the wind.

"Why my car?"

She heard the second speaker clearly: Ian.

Only the tops of the men's heads were visible as they walked down the side path towards the front of the house. What was Ian doing out there at this time of night?

She heard the familiar bang of the front door of Vesey Villa and then the sound of people coming upstairs. She went over to her door and listened. They had paused outside Ian's flat and then she heard a key in the lock. Sandra put the chain across her door and prepared to open it. Her heart was thumping. Ian was up to no good. He was no better than all the other dodgy males there'd been in her life. She wanted to know what dirty business he was involved in.

Slowly she opened the door a couple of centimetres and peered on to the landing. There was no one there. She opened it as far as the chain would allow.

Ian came out of the flat first. He was dressed only in shirt sleeves and looked half-mad. He kept glancing behind him and then touching his neck and examining his fingers. Ignatius followed him. As they turned towards bedsit two, Sandra closed her door and leaned against it. Whatever was happening, Ian and Ignatius were in it together. No wonder he hadn't wanted her or Amy to go to the police. She went back to the window and looked out again. It was still slightly open.

"Lift her up!"

Ignatius was giving the orders.

It was a person, not a carpet! Could it be Maxine? Shaking, Sandra crept into Halifax's sleeping alcove to look out of the window facing the parking area at the front of the house. The boot of Ian's car was open.

"Curl her around slightly and then she'll fit." The words were faint but audible through the ill-fitting window frame.

Once the body was stowed the two men got in the car. Sandra thought Ian was driving. And they were definitely using his car. She tried to rationalise her thoughts. Something bad was going on. The two men were driving a body away in the middle of the night. They were supposed to have no connection to each other, apart from inhabiting the same flat at different times.

There was no question about what Sandra had to do next. She called the police. She told them what she'd seen and gave them Ian's car registration. She'd learned it off by heart when she was in full stupid-teenager-crush mode. Then she allowed herself a few deep breaths before checking that Halifax was still safely in the Land of Nod. Then there was another phone call to make.

"Amy? It's all kicking off here."

There were a few sleepy grunts and mumbles before Sandra had the other girl's full attention.

"I've just called the police and this time I think they'll take things seriously."

She explained what had happened, including what a fool she'd been to allow herself to be taken in by Ian's charm.

"They must be in it together," she said. "I think they're moving Maxine's body."

There was no coherent reply from Amy, only the sound of sobbing.

"Are you still there?" Sandra asked.

"She really is dead, then. I hoped I might have got it wrong." The girl's words were thick with tears. "What am I going to tell her mum?"

"Amy, can you get a taxi round here? We need to be sure of things before we tell anyone else. Don't contact Maxine's mum until we have proper information from the police. You shouldn't be alone right now and I don't want to be. Please come round."

"I'll call a cab."

Sandra paced up and down. Then she got dressed.

Every now and again she crept alongside Halifax's bed and looked out of the window to see if the police had arrived.

The taxi came first and Sandra went downstairs to open the front door before Amy could press the buzzer and waken Halifax. Seconds later, two police cars arrived. After a brief word with Sandra, one team of men headed for the back garden and the other set off in the direction Ian's car had taken.

Sandra and Amy sat sipping cocoa, sobbing and whispering.

**

Ian followed Ignatius' directions with the sharp vegetable knife resting on the skin of his neck. Twice he missed a turning because he was given the instruction too late and three times Ignatius decided they were going the wrong way and made him perform a hasty U turn.

"You're worse than a woman at navigating," Ian muttered.

"Shut it." The knife blade nicked his skin. "And drive faster."

Ian put his foot down a little. "Where are we going?"

"The river. Drive, don't ask questions."

The roads were almost empty. Only the occasional car passed them in the opposite direction. Ian flashed his headlights at one but it drove onwards. Perhaps he should swerve in front of the next car and bring this nightmare charade to an end.

Another sharp nick in the neck warned him not to try anything.

They seemed to drive miles and miles from the city. Fear had shut down all but the essential parts of Ian's mind. Only the odd signpost registered with him. He knew they were somewhere in Derbyshire.

"Next left."

There were no streetlamps and the road was a series of blind bends. Ian switched to full-beam but Ignatius immediately flicked it off again. After five hundred yards of closely hedged lanes, the tarmac ended and the river suddenly appeared in Ian's headlights, shining and rippling.

Ignatius instructed him to reverse the car towards the water. He contemplated going too far so the vehicle would end up in the river, but he didn't have the guts to put himself at risk. Without the headlights it was pitch black. Illuminated by Ignatius's torch they lifted Maxine from the boot.

"We need to wade in," said Ignatius, "and let her go in the middle of the river so the current takes her downstream. I don't want her found here, though it's your tyre marks they'll find so you'll be in the frame for her murder."

The shock of the icy water made Ian gasp. Ignatius moved quickly towards the centre of the flow, seemingly oblivious to the temperature. Ian was dragged with him as he clutched the other end of Maxine's body. They were in up to chest height before Ignatius gave the order to let the girl go. In a few seconds the gruesome black parcel was out of sight.

Then Ian made another break for freedom. He lunged after the body and started to swim. But Ignatius merely put out his arms and caught Ian's legs. Ian kicked against him but his head went under the water and terror made him stop struggling. He concentrated on finding the strength to get his head above the surface.

Ignatius pulled him back to the shore by his legs and

then transferred his grip to Ian's right arm. He pushed him against the car.

"You know too much. I have to kill you now."

Ian was shaking uncontrollably. The words were barely making sense. Terror and cold had paralysed his mind and body. He was unable to function. Something sharp nicked his neck.

"Are you deaf? Your body will be going in the river too."

He felt a hard slap across his face and then another one.

***

It had only just occurred to Ignatius that his lack of planning had left him with no option but to kill Ian Wolvestone. Otherwise the man would go straight to the police. He must be stabbed and dumped in the river to follow Maxine downstream.

His victim's eyes were fixed on the knife. Ignatius prodded the blade experimentally at his chest. Ian whimpered.

"Let me go. You'll have plenty of time to escape before I get anywhere near the police. Take my car. I've got no phone and I'm in the middle of nowhere."

Ignatius shifted his gaze from his victim's chest to his throat. He remembered strangling Maxine. Ian was the same height as him and would fight back. It had to be the knife. There would be a lot of blood, a warm, gushing, incriminating, crimson liquid, which would shoot all over Ignatius and make him smell like a slaughterhouse.

"I've got a son." Ian's voice was shaky. "He lives with his mum but I think about him all the time."

I think about him all the time. He talks about you all the time. A switch flicked in Ignatius' brain.

"Does he make you proud?"

"Absolutely."

Ignatius could feel tears in his eyes.

"I almost had a son."

"Perhaps you know how I feel then. Please don't make my son suffer."

Ignatius thought about the missing white plastic stick. He saw Maxine's face when she told him his baby was dead. He remembered how it felt to kill her. Her death had been justifiable.

"How old is your boy?"

"Seven."

Give me a child until he is seven and I will give you the man. Unless a female gets hold of him. Killing this father would leave his son in the clutches of the mother and lead to another wasted life like his own. Ignatius lowered the hand with the knife.

"Keep your mouth shut about tonight."

He watched Ian's silhouette stumble away into the dark and head towards the road. Then he got into the car and started the engine. But he didn't drive. He sat and stared at the windscreen as it slowly steamed up with his breath. He had no plan.

The adrenaline of the evening began to fade as he realised his predicament. It was only a matter of time before Ian got to the police and then his description would be circulated to every cop in the country. Ignatius ground his teeth and gripped the steering wheel. He leaned forward and cleared the windscreen with the sleeve of his jacket and then started to drive.

Without thinking, he was back on the A38 and heading towards Birmingham. Coherent thoughts emerged slowly from his muddled mind. He needed cash. Since Ignatius had quit his job, his bank account had dwindled to almost nothing. The only thing left was

Maxine's debit card. At the moment the police didn't have her body. They didn't know for certain she was dead. He'd cleverly laid a trail indicating she was in Derby but possibly going further afield for a time. So if anyone checked her account it would seem natural that she'd withdraw a large sum of money prior to departure.

Ignatius pressed harder on the accelerator. He'd bypass Birmingham and carry on south. Fleetingly, he thought of Betty waiting for her bread and milk. Then he pushed her from his mind. Surely the nurse would make sure she had enough food.

The road was empty. It was pointless sticking to speed limits. A road sign indicated he was approaching Lichfield. The car started to sputter. Ignatius pushed the pedal to the floor. There was no response. Now the scenery was passing more slowly. There was time to notice a cat staring at him from its perch on a fence. Ignatius returned the stare. He willed the evil-eyed creature to topple backwards. Nothing happened.

Nothing happened either as he pumped the accelerator. He could read every word of the 'For Sale' notice stuck in the rear window of a parked car. Ian's car stopped of its own free will fifty yards further down the road.

"Bastard!" Ignatius slammed his fist down on the plastic covering the fuel gauge. "Mean bastard! Why didn't he keep the tank full?"

He got out of the Mondeo and walked around it, kicking each of the four tyres in turn. His aggression built with each explosive blow. The physical pain as his already sore toe hit hard rubber sent his anger to volcanic levels. Someone would damn well suffer for this.

Dawn was seeping into the night sky. Before long the

road would be busy with commuters and the car would be spotted. Ignatius couldn't afford the luxury of planning his revenge right now. He brought his fist down heavily on the car roof and then started walking along the grass verge.

When he reached Lichfield, a few people were already starting their day around the town. Ignatius pulled up his hood and hurried. At the cashpoint he glanced around several times, wondering if there was CCTV. He tried to burrow the bottom half of his face into his jacket and wished he had dark glasses.

The machine requested Maxine's PIN. Ignatius hesitated. She'd told him it only once. They'd wanted late night chips and neither of them had any cash.

"Your turn to pay for a change," he'd said.

"1234." She handed him a plastic card.

"Moron! That's a pathetic PIN."

Her voice had gone defensive and the shadow of a sulk passed over her face.

"It means I can remember it."

"You should change it."

There was a woman behind him now, waiting to get cash. He could sense her impatience. She probably had a job to get to and a normal day in front of her. The PIN request message was still on the screen. Ignatius typed the digits and crossed his fingers. Maxine seldom did what she was told. He prayed that his advice to change the PIN had been no exception to the rule.

A few seconds later the machine spewed out ten £20 notes. Ignatius shoved them into his pocket. He almost bumped into the woman behind him as he turned to walk away with his head down.

Next he had to get away from Lichfield, the dumped car and the cash withdrawal. He headed towards the station, stopping at a discount store that had just opened. From the stand of cheap reading glasses he selected the weakest pair, and then he chose a black woollen hat and a red scarf. All fugitives needed a disguise in case a camera caught them or an observant ticket collector spotted them.

London was the obvious destination. He could melt into the crowds of the big city and never be found. But £200 wouldn't go far in the capital. A few nights in a dingy Bed and Breakfast and the money would be gone. He needed to lie low for longer.

His mother had had a friend who used to visit them from Milton Keynes. Her name was Kathleen or Karen. They'd worked together before Ignatius was born. She'd started coming once a year after his dad died and stayed for the week. At first she came by coach and moaned about travel sickness. It was the same monologue every time she arrived and his mother served her tea and chocolate digestives.

"No biscuits for me. Not until my stomach's settled. Coach drivers should be shot. The way they take those corners! They've no consideration for their passengers."

The last time Kathleen or Karen came was for his mother's funeral. She'd cornered him at the wake.

"No need to watch my stomach this time," she said indicating her plate piled with sandwiches and a slab of rich fruit cake. "I got the train to Lichfield and then on to here. Gentle as sailing on a duck pond. I wish I'd discovered it whilst your mother was alive."

Ignatius decided to put Kathleen or Karen's tip into action and take the train to Milton Keynes. There was nothing to connect him to that town so no one would think of looking for him there.

He donned his disguise and went to buy a ticket.

Chapter Sixteen

After a mammoth trudge, street lights appeared out of the darkness and the outlines of buildings became visible. Ian banged on the door of the first house he came to. He hammered and hammered without stopping to listen for movement within. When the door was pulled open he almost fell on top of a man in a dressing-gown.

"Police! Call the police," Ian said, clutching at the door frame to steady himself. Cold, tiredness and fear had stolen his ability to be coherent. "He dumped her body and almost killed me."

"What?"

"The police. Hurry up!"

The man dialled 999. Then the two men stood in the hall with the front door wide-open and waited. When the man's wife called down the stairs he told her to stay where she was and not let the kids out of their rooms. Gradually, Ian realised that the man didn't believe his story. He thought Ian was a conman or a criminal. Ian was shaking with cold and unable to explain further, so they both stood in the icy blast of night air for the fifteen minutes it took the police to arrive.

It was warm in the police station but Ian couldn't

stop shivering, shaking and crying. They sat him at a table and asked questions that he struggled to understand. Finally they sent for a doctor who ordered a hot drink, dry clothes and a few minutes' peace. He examined the nicks and cuts Ignatius had inflicted and declared them superficial.

The police offered Ian a lawyer but he refused. Waiting for a lawyer would slow things down and he wanted this whole episode finished so he could go home. Sitting in a weird, oversized blue overall in exchange for his wet clothes, he told them everything that had happened. They showed him a map and he pointed as best he could to where he thought the body had gone into the water, based on the signage he'd noticed at the end of his journey.

"You say Ignatius Smith escaped in your car. Where would he go?"

"I've no idea."

After what felt like hours they let him go.

"We'll need to talk to you again," the policeman in charge said, "but you can go for now. We'll keep your clothes for forensics. And you can't go back to the flat; it's a crime scene. Have you got someone you can stay with?"

Sandra and Josephine were the only people in the city he knew. Neither was kindly disposed towards him. One still carried a grudge about something that had happened in the past and the other he'd wrongly led on to believe they could have a future together.

"No one. If I could have my wallet from the flat I could go to a hotel."

He was allowed nothing from the flat until the next day but they drove him to a hotel for what remained of the night.

Sandra had phoned in sick for the first time ever. She didn't feel able to serve lattes and cappuccinos to weary supermarket shoppers. She and Amy had sat up until the police activity around Vesey Villa had quietened. At around 5:30 a.m. they'd caught a couple of hours sleep in armchairs before the alarm clock sounded and Sandra had had to get Halifax off to school.

Later she'd walked Amy to the bus stop and they'd promised to keep in touch about events. When she got back, the police were waiting for her. She and Amy had already told them a lot during the night. Now the same two officers wanted to go over it all again.

"We have to warn you that Ignatius Smith is still at large," the policewoman said, closing her notebook. "If he comes back here don't approach him. Call us straight away. Or dial 999."

"You think he's dangerous?"

Sandra was scared. Ignatius had murdered his girlfriend and he might kill again.

"We expect to apprehend him soon. Don't worry."

The policewoman smiled and patted Sandra on the shoulder.

After they'd gone Sandra went back to bed but sleep was impossible. As soon as she closed her eyes she saw Ian's face and then she was forced to go back over the last ten days and realise how gullible she'd been to fall for someone in league with a killer. It was just as well he'd ended their relationship before it began.

Sandra needed to erase Ian from her mind and channel the nervous energy currently pulsing through her body into getting her own future sorted out. She picked up the well-thumbed college prospectus from the dining table. Still she wasn't sure she was clever enough to learn something new or pass an exam. But the prospect of her and Halifax being stuck in Vesey Villa indefinitely was far worse than the fear of being the dunce of the class. It was time to stop procrastinating. She wrapped a scarf around her hair, put her coat on and went for the bus.

"Classes started back in September so you've already missed a few weeks," the college receptionist said when Sandra asked about enrolling. "Take a seat and I'll see if we've got any spaces."

There were two plastic chairs in the small waiting area and one was already occupied by a man in his twenties with an expensive-looking camera. Sandra sat next to him.

"Are you doing a photography course?" she asked.

"No, I'm a reporter for the Evening Mail. I'm here to cover a new apprenticeship scheme that the college are involved in. What about you?"

"The usual story. I didn't try at school so now I've got to get qualifications the hard way."

"I admire you for biting the bullet and having a go."

Sandra warmed to the friendly twinkle in the reporter's eye. She told him about the better life she hoped to achieve for herself and Halifax. He was a good listener and it was easier to talk to a stranger about her aspirations than it was to justify her actions to Donna or her other girlfriends.

"I wish you luck," the reporter said when he was called away to do his interview. "Here's my business card and perhaps one day I'll be doing a story about your success."

Sandra took the small card and laughed at the ridiculous suggestion about him reporting on her success, but he'd left her feeling positive and also slightly regretful that she wouldn't see him again. She took the registration forms from the receptionist for the courses with vacancies and promised to complete and return them quickly.

Back at Vesey Villa she couldn't settle down to form-filling. Anxious, she got up and looked out of the front window to see if the police were still prowling around. A taxi stopped outside. Ian got out and stared upwards, directly at her. He lifted his hand and waved. She didn't respond, but her heart looped the loop. She couldn't control her emotions but she could and would control her outward response to him.

When she heard the knock at the door of her flat she knew it was him. Against her better judgement she let him in.

"They're allowing me to take some stuff from the flat," he said. "I can't go around dressed like this for much longer." He gestured to the odd overalls he was wearing. "My stuff was soaking wet but they've taken it off to forensics anyway."

"Have they arrested you?"

"No. Why would they?"

"So you spun them some tale then? Just like you managed to persuade me you were all sweetness and light?"

"I haven't persuaded anybody of anything. I told the police the truth. And I haven't lied to you either."

He sank down on to the settee.

"Don't make yourself at home - you're not stopping."

Ian stood up again and moved towards her.

"You don't believe me, do you? You think I'm actually mixed up in Maxine's murder? What possible motive could I have?"

He looked tired and worn down.

"See what Ignatius did to me to make me help him."

He pointed to the cuts and scratches on his neck. "He held a knife against me the whole time. It was my own vegetable knife."

Sandra said nothing. He took hold of both her arms and looked into her face.

"I'm innocent, Sandra. Please believe me."

Despite the doubts, her heart was doing strange things. She wanted to hold him close. She wanted to be held close. She wanted to kiss him. But he was getting back with his wife and she had responsibilities. She couldn't afford to get mixed up with a criminal. Sandra had been cheated on and lied to in the past and she would never allow it to happen to her again.

"Prove to me you're not in league with Ignatius in any way, shape or form."

"How?"

"Tell me what you told the police."

"Can I sit down? I've hardly slept."

"Join the club."

Ian sat on the settee and Sandra placed herself on a dining chair. She listened to the story of the foxes howling and Ian looking out and seeing Ignatius. He told her how he'd been forced to help at knife-point and use his own car.

"They found my car abandoned on the A38 and Ignatius's car is in forensics now. It had a flat battery, apparently, and they think that may be partly why he dragged me into this."

"So you dumped that poor girl in the river just because he said so?"

"What would you have done? She was already dead. If I'd protested I'd have been dead too, leaving Marcus without a father. Would you have risked your life to save a dead body? Would you have left Halifax without a mum?"

"I suppose not. But how was he going to stop you spilling the beans afterwards?"

Ian explained how Ignatius had been about to kill him but then, all of a sudden, when Marcus was mentioned, he'd seemed to soften. Then he'd let him go.

"It was odd. He said he nearly had a son. How can you nearly have a son?"

Sandra had no idea what to think, never mind wonder how Ignatius had almost had a son. Should she really believe that Ian had been forced at knife-point to move Maxine's body and the killer had then let him go?

"All this has taught me something." Ian was standing over her now and his eyes were melting her insides. "I want us to start again. I realise now that life is for living, not making convoluted plans for the future or wasting time hoping that things outside my control might eventually come right. No matter what I do, Josephine will never forgive me for Amsterdam. She doesn't seem to care if I go off to Dubai for a year. In fact, I get the impression she'd like me to. I want to be with a woman I like and respect; someone who feels the same way about me as I do about them. That woman is you."

Sandra looked at Ian in his funny overalls. She no longer knew which way was up.

"Are you going to Dubai?"

"No. There'll be other jobs."

"I'm sorry, Ian. I can't be second choice after your ex-wife."

"What?" Every muscle in his face wilted. "I thought we were on the same wavelength."

"Me too. But I wasn't good enough for you, was I? Now you claim to have suddenly 'seen the light'." Her hands put apostrophes around the last three words. "How do I know that in a couple of months the novelty of having a 'bit of rough' won't wear off? I've got Halifax to consider. I don't want her exposed to a string of short-term relationships. That's why I've not dated much."

"Sandra, I've never seen you as a 'bit of rough'. I want you to know that. I'm not going to beg but if you change your mind, this is where I'm staying."

Ian handed her the address of his hotel and left.

Fifteen minutes later, Sandra went to collect Halifax from school. There was no sign of Ian or his taxi but the police were still in the garden. Halifax had been scared that morning when she'd seen the panda cars in the front and policemen all around. But Sandra had reassured her with a confidence dug from nowhere and said they should look on it as an adventure or pretend they were part of a TV crime programme.

The girl was back to her usual bouncy self when she came running out of school.

"I told them about the police in Circle Time," she gabbled. "Miss Firth said not to frighten everyone but I told them it wasn't frightening but very interesting and exciting. Are the policemen still there, Mum?"

"Yes, they've been busy looking for clues all day."

"I'm going to be a policewoman when I grow up and catch all the bad people."

"You'll be brilliant at it!" said Sandra.

She hoped her daughter would have a change of heart as she got older. A police officer's job was tough and dangerous.

"Can we go to the playground with Marcus and his daddy?"

"No. Marcus is with his mum today."

"I wish I had a daddy like Marcus has."

Sandra bent and gave her daughter a hug.

"Me too," she whispered.

Halifax wriggled free. "So why don't you marry him?"

"I … we … We don't know each other well enough."

"Next time we see him I'm going to ask him to take you on a date."

Sandra didn't reply. She unlocked the bedsit and Halifax ran in, dumping her coat and grabbing an apple. As Sandra chopped an onion for their lentil curry she found real tears mixing with those triggered by the vegetable. Both Ian and Halifax thought they'd make a good couple. She herself thought they'd be great together. So why was she holding back?

Fear.

Her romantic history was a tale of failure and now she had another person's heart to consider as well as her own. Halifax liked Ian. She'd be devastated if somewhere down the line he rejected them both or if he got carted off to prison on a murder charge.

Sandra warmed the plates and naan bread under the grill.

"Alicia's kitten died yesterday. It got run over," her daughter said.

"Is Alicia very sad?"

"Yes, she cried when she told us at Circle Time, but Miss Firth said it was better to have loved and lost than never to have loved at all."

"And did Alicia agree with that?"

"Yes. She was glad she'd had a cat for a few months rather than never had one."

"That's a very grown-up way of looking at things."

"Me and Alicia are very grown-up."

As Sandra washed the dishes she glanced at the piece of paper Ian had left. She recognised the name of the hotel. It was on the outskirts of the city, a bus ride away.

"Get your coat," she said as she dried the last plate. "We're going to put Miss Firth's motto to the test."

"What?"

"It's better to have loved and lost than never to have loved at all. We're going to see Ian."

***

The train journey confirmed to Ignatius why he and most other people preferred the autonomy of driving metal boxes at speed down the motorway to 'green' public transport. The trains to Milton Keynes were not frequent and, after buying his ticket, he discovered he'd just missed one. The next was cancelled due to staff sickness and the one after that was running extremely late and was further delayed by leaves on the line.

Ignatius curbed his urge to rant and rave at the man in the ticket office, the woman walking through the train who called herself the 'train manager', or anyone else who'd listen. Causing a fuss would draw attention. Instead, he pounced on a discarded newspaper and struggled to focus on the words through his new glasses. Eventually he took them off because the paper hid his face anyway.

Walking out of the station in Milton Keynes, Ignatius had a curious 'on holiday' feeling. He was in a new and unexplored town. It could be a foreign land. There were taxis, buses and roads in front of him, each offering unknown opportunities. But there was no package holiday rep to usher him safely on to a coach and to care if he went missing.

It was an effort to concentrate on what to do next. His brain felt fuzzy from lack of sleep and food. His stomach growled. Ignatius realised he hadn't eaten for twenty-four hours and had drunk nothing but a can of coke purchased from the discount store. He turned and went back into the station, following the scent of coffee.

The board behind the takeaway counter listed confusing permutations of coffee types and sizes. Maxine had been the one for fancy drinks. Ignatius just wanted a method of ingesting caffeine to kick-start his brain. A large latte was what she always asked for when he was paying, so he ordered the same now. It came in an oversized cardboard cup with a plastic lid. He emptied three sachets of brown sugar into the drink before even tasting it. Then he took a sip and added another sachet. The sugar supplied his body with energy at no extra cost.

Ignatius stood in the main station concourse as he refuelled. He could see nowhere to sit and gather his thoughts or plan what to do next. Everyone around him was moving. They strode purposefully either towards or from trains. No one was standing in limbo like him.

A policeman walked in through the main doors. Ignatius raised the coffee cup to cover his face and turned towards the wall. The officer paused and scanned the concourse. A police car was visible outside and another drew up just behind it.

Ignatius' heart started pounding. He pretended to be studying the Arrivals and Departures board. The glasses were slipping down his nose. He pushed them back up with his free hand and then pulled his hat further down. Out of the corner of his eye he watched the policeman walk slowly past the ticket counters. Then another blue uniform came into the concourse and began walking among the people hanging round the coffee shop and newsagents.

"Excuse me."

The second officer was at his side.

"Sorry," Ignatius said through the wool of his scarf. He stepped aside.

Both policemen completed a circuit of the station and left.

Coffee slopped over his wrist and Ignatius realised his hand was shaking. He moved to the station's glass front and looked out. The police cars had gone. The taxis were queuing for fares in an orderly fashion, inching forward as the front car took a passenger and drove away.

On a ledge in front of him was a pile of business cards. He picked one up. The front pictured a small house with the words 'Bed and Breakfast' printed across it. On the back of the card was an address and phone number. Ignatius took out his mobile and switched it on. This had been another of Maxine's fancy ideas. He hardly used the thing and wondered if there'd be enough battery or credit to make a call.

"Comfort Stay Bed and Breakfast. Can I help you?"

A woman's voice.

"How much for a single room?"

"£35 per night with continental breakfast or £40 with full English."

Ignatius' mouth began to water at the thought of a full English breakfast with sausage and bacon and beans and …. But he needed be careful with money. The police might put a stop on Maxine's account at any minute.

"Is there a discount for cash or stays longer than one night?"

Ignatius felt pleased at thinking up the question. The coffee had done the trick in sharpening his brain. There was a short pause at the other end. It sounded as though pages were being turned in a book.

"We're very quiet at the moment. I can do you seven

191

nights for £140 with continental breakfast."

"Make it an English breakfast and it's a deal."

The woman was reluctant but agreed.

It was a two mile walk to the guest house but the landlady had given clear instructions. She answered the door almost as soon as he rang the bell. At the small reception desk she gave him a registration form.

"Cold out, is it?" she asked, indicating his woolly hat and the scarf wrapped over the bottom half of his face. "You won't need them in here. This is a centrally heated establishment."

Ignatius realised he was drawing more attention to himself by keeping his disguise on than by removing it. He took them off and then bent over the form.

"You can do it in your room if you like and give it to me at breakfast in the morning. You're in room three on the first floor. Where's your luggage?"

"I'm travelling light."

She gave him an odd look and showed him to his room.

"Bathroom's down the landing. Breakfast's at eight."

The room contained two single beds, a wardrobe, sink and a kettle on a hospitality tray. Alongside the teabags there was a pack of three custard creams and another of three bourbon biscuits. He ate them all. Then he visited the bathroom before closing the curtains and going to sleep fully clothed.

***

Ian watched darkness fall outside the hotel window. After Sandra's rejection he'd sat in his room without even the energy to remove the police overalls. Now his stomach was complaining and he realised he'd had nothing to eat since a room service breakfast many

192

hours earlier. He should think about going out and finding food.

He turned on the shower. It was hot and powerful. He stood underneath the pounding water, letting it cleanse him of everything that had happened the night before. It was his first shower since moving to Vesey Villa and he used the entire complimentary mini bottle of shower gel.

He towelled himself dry and then put on the clean clothes he'd been allowed to rescue from the bedsit. Before he had chance to find his shoes and check his wallet for cash his phone rang. Josephine's name came up on the display. She must have found out about last night. Perhaps it had been on the news.

"Hello," he said. "It's not what …"

"Can we talk? Please, Ian. I've been thinking about what you said about reconciliation and Dubai."

"I …"

"I'm on my way to the flat now. Marcus is with me."

"No! Don't go there. I'm not at the flat. I'm in a hotel. You haven't seen the news?"

"No."

"Are you on speaker phone?"

A spark of Josephine's old tetchiness returned.

"Yes. As I said, I'm driving."

"I'll tell you later. For now just come to this hotel." He gave her the address.

"We're not far away," she said. "We'll be there in two minutes."

Ian went down to reception to meet them.

"Dad!"

Marcus raced across the reception area and flung himself on his father. Ian crouched down and gave his son a bear hug. Josephine looked around the busy hotel lobby.

"Can we go somewhere quieter?"

Ian took them up to his room. Marcus pounced on the complimentary pack of biscuits.

"There's only two." He looked from one parent to another.

"Not for me," said Josephine.

Ian ignored his empty stomach.

"You have them both and stick the TV on. Your mother and I have got some boring stuff to talk about."

For once, no one told Marcus to turn the volume down and sit further away from the screen.

"You wanted to talk about reconciliation?" Ian asked in a hushed voice. "I thought you wanted me to go to Dubai?"

"Marcus never stops talking about you. I realise now he'd be heartbroken if you went. He's desperate to have a proper dad again. He keeps asking if you can come and live with us."

"But what about you? Do you want me back? Can we put Amsterdam behind us?"

Ian looked into the eyes of the woman who'd shared a large part of his life. She'd seen him mature from a nineteen-year-old student to a grown man. She knew all about his habits, likes and dislikes. She also knew the very worst things about him. Sandra had fallen for the initial outward impression he gave, whereas if Josephine took him back, it would be an informed decision.

"I want the old you back. I want the pre-Amsterdam you that I can trust. But if you go to Dubai, how will I know what you're doing there?"

She took hold of his hands.

"I want to come back and, if you can bear me being unemployed a bit longer, I'd prefer not to go to Dubai. My place is with you and Marcus."

As if reading each other's minds, they both leant

forward to kiss for the first time since that incriminating Facebook post. Marcus bounced on to the bed between his parents and grinned.

"Are there any more biscuits, Dad?"

"He's hungry. We haven't eaten yet," said Josephine, snapping instantly back into 'mother' mode. "Why don't we go out for a meal and you can tell us why you're staying here instead of at the bedsit."

"Yes! Let's go for pizza!" Marcus bounced again.

Ian's stomach agreed with his son. He put his arm around Marcus and held him tightly until his mobile rang again. He glanced at the screen. It was Sandra. He answered the call as nonchalantly as he could.

"Me and Halifax are in the hotel reception," she said immediately. "The bloke behind the counter wouldn't give me your room number. He looked at me as though I was trailer trash."

"I'll be right down." Then he turned to Josephine. "I just need to have a word with someone downstairs. Stick the kettle on and make yourselves at home. I'll see if I can talk reception into giving me some more biscuits."

Ian took the stairs down the three floors to reception. His head filled with the possibility of finally putting Amsterdam behind him and re-building his life with Josephine. Then he paused mid-step. Sandra wouldn't have come here on a mere social call. Her visit must have a purpose. When he got to the lobby, she and Halifax were standing by the hotel entrance looking awkward.

Sandra gave a tentative wave and glanced at the man behind the reception desk before walking towards Ian. The receptionist was expressionless, but it was obvious that in his opinion Sandra and Halifax didn't belong in this establishment. Sandra had the purple scarf tied around her hair and dark green leggings clung to her slim thighs. The outfit was completed by black Doc Martens and a navy jacket. She looked very sexy. Halifax, like Marcus, was still in her school uniform.

"I shouldn't have come here." The words tumbled out of Sandra as soon as she reached Ian. "We don't fit just like we won't fit with the rest of your life. I should've torn up the address of this place and tossed it in the bin. Like what you'll do with me and Halifax when you're bored."

Ian said nothing. His feelings were confused. Both Josephine and Sandra had rejected him and now they'd both changed their minds. Simultaneously

Sandra's eyes were darting around as though she expected to be thrown out at any minute.

"I bet wish you wish you'd never left me the address of this place."

Ian stepped closer and stroked her cheek.

"There are things in my life that I regret but that's not one of them."

Sandra's eyes widened.

"Really?"

"Are you going to take my mum on a date?" Halifax's voice was loud in the hushed reception area. "Do you fancy her? Will you be my daddy?"

Ian was suddenly aware of being the centre of attention. There was a titter from two elderly ladies drinking coffee at a low table. The male receptionist was nudging a female counterpart who'd appeared beside him.

"Halifax!" Sandra stepped back from Ian and placed her finger on her daughter's lips to quieten her. Then she glanced back up at him, her eyes shining with expectation.

Ian felt wretched. Josephine was upstairs with his

son, offering the three of them a new start as a family. Vivacious, delightful Sandra was in front of him - waiting, and deserving, to be treated like a lady.

There was no question about the choice Ian was going to make. The words he had to say were the hardest he'd ever uttered.

"Josephine's willing to trust me again."

The look of hope on Sandra's face vanished, her lips twisted and she swallowed hard.

"She turned up out of the blue with Marcus just a few minutes ago."

"Go back to them, Ian." Her voice was flat. "And NEVER contact me again. It's cruel to lead me on and then reject me. You've done it TWICE. You're not the man I thought you were."

"Sandra, everything I said to you before about us being together... I meant them, but things got turned upside down when Josephine arrived. Under different circumstances I'd be with you in a shot."

"Don't flannel me. It doesn't work. You were keeping me in reserve. Second choice."

"Sandra! I promise - the feelings I have for you were, are genuine."

"I understand. She's from the right social class and I'm not fit to lick her shoes."

"No! Listen, Sandra, earlier when I invited you to come round here if you changed your mind about me, about us, things were different."

"Even then I was second choice. I'm a fool to think I could ever have meant anything to you."

Ian hung his head, realising the truth in Sandra's words.

"You do what you think's best," said Sandra taking Halifax's hand and preparing to leave.

"Doesn't Ian want to be my daddy?"

Halifax's voice carried across the lobby as they headed for the door. Ian swallowed the lump in his throat and headed back upstairs to his family.

Chapter Seventeen

"Turn this rubbish off, please!"

"Mum, it's not rubbish. Dad watched Dr Who when he was a little …"

"I don't care what your father did. You've got homework to do."

"Dad, tell her, will you? Tell her I'm allowed to watch the TV."

Father and son sat close together on the settee sharing an illicit bar of chocolate as they watched the Daleks. Ian shoved the chocolate in his pocket and shrugged his shoulders.

"I had to do homework, too, when I was a boy. How about I record the rest of the programme and we watch it later?"

Marcus gave an exaggerated sigh and uncurled himself to a standing position.

"You've got an hour," Josephine said, "and then dinner will be ready."

The boy clumped upstairs.

"Don't look at me as if I'm some sort of ogre. Watching TV all night won't get him to university."

"It's not just that."

Ian looked at the floor, then the ceiling. He fiddled

with his hands.

"Spit it out."

He was trying to phrase what he wanted to say so it didn't sound as if he was finding fault.

"It feels as though you're always trying to keep us on the go. Marcus and I aren't free to relax at all. Whenever we snatch a few moments together you find something that one or other of us has to do: me emptying the bins, Marcus tidying his room…"

"But …"

Ian held his hand up to silence her.

"I know they're all jobs that need doing. But much of the time they're not urgent. They could wait until the TV programme's over or we've finished our game of chess, or whatever it is."

"You and he …"

He shook his head at her and ploughed on.

"It feels as if you don't want Marcus and me to build a close relationship." Ian placed his hand gently on his ex-wife's shoulder. "You're his mother and I'd never try to push you out, but togetherness with him is what I dreamed of all the time we were living apart. I want to make the most of this chance to have a real presence in my son's life."

"It's been just Marcus and me for longer than the three of us were a family. It's hard to adjust from the responsibility of being in sole charge to sharing things."

He pulled her close but she was tense in his arms.

"Let me in please, Josephine. Sometimes I think we're nearly there, and then you pull the shutters down again."

"I just need time. I'm trying my best, really I am, Ian. What we had before … before Amsterdam was good. But it will take time for me to trust that you won't … do it again."

Ian sighed. Amsterdam was the only thing in his life he truly regretted.

"Shall we go back to the beginning and start with a date? Josephine, please will you come out to dinner with me tomorrow night?"

She gave him a puzzled look.

"O.K. Yes, please. I'd like to go out to dinner with you."

No one had said the attempt at reconciliation would be easy but Ian was willing to move heaven and earth to get his ex-wife to fall in love with him again, for Marcus's sake as well as his own.

Sandra still featured heavily in his thoughts. Being with her had been easy. There was no past to create a barrier between them. Their relationship had started with a clean sheet and no regrets. That scenario had its attractions. But he pushed her purple-framed face from his mind. He would never forget Sandra and he hoped that she'd find someone to care for her and treat her like the true lady she was.

He'd been back to the bedsit earlier in the day to collect the rest of his stuff; the police had finished their evidence-gathering. He'd paused outside bedsit two, his fist raised and ready to knock. He longed to see her impish face and the wisps of that odd-coloured hair she'd dyed especially for him. But it would have been cruel to call on her. It had to be a clean break. So he'd let his hand drop, loaded up the car and disappeared from her life for ever.

*****

Marcus was in his pyjamas when they left on their date.

"You're all dressed up!" he exclaimed to them when they kissed him goodnight. "You look like a proper mummy and daddy who love each other."

"Of course we love each other," Josephine said.

She was wearing a knee length red jersey dress that clung revealingly to her slim figure and showed just the right amount of cleavage. Ian had chosen khaki chinos and a cream open-necked shirt.

"Now remember, Buster stays in the utility whilst we're out. No sneaking him on to your bed."

Josephine re-fastened Marcus's pyjama jacket. He'd got the buttons in the wrong holes.

"You look wonderful, Mrs Wolvestone," Ian whispered as they got into her car.

"You don't scrub up badly yourself," she said with an approving look. "By the way, it's Ms Pilkington now."

"I hope to persuade you to change it back again. Soon."

"Slowly, please Ian. Our marriage may have been destroyed in one night but it will take a lot longer to rebuild it."

At the restaurant he persuaded the Italian waiter to seat them at a corner table where they'd get some privacy.

"You're better at wine than I am," he said, handing her the list. "We'll get a taxi home and I'll walk back for the car tomorrow."

Josephine opened her mouth as if she was about to argue. Then she thought better of it and went back to the wine list. Ian wondered absently what Sandra would make of a place like this. Would she have anything suitable to wear? He remembered his promise to take her out for a proper meal. Was she disappointed it had never materialised?

"Penny for them?"

Josephine was staring at him.

"Have you ordered the wine?"

"Yes, but you were glazed over and somewhere else completely. What were you thinking about?"

"Just that not everybody gets a second chance in life and I really need to make it work this time."

The evening was pleasant. They talked a lot about Marcus; he was a safe subject.

After sharing a bottle of wine and a couple of brandies they were nicely mellow. In the taxi on the way home Ian put his arm around Josephine. She didn't protest or try and wriggle away. He pulled her closer and she rested her head on his shoulder. He didn't remember them sitting like that since they'd first started going out. The lemon scent of her shampoo was fresh and her close warmth made him hope that tonight they might build a bridge between their bedrooms. They hadn't shared a bed since Josephine had found out about Amsterdam.

He paid the driver as Josephine went inside to check that all was well with the babysitter.

"Yes, we had a lovely time," Josephine was saying to her friend when Ian walked in. "Pleasant surroundings, good food and excellent company."

She looked at him and smiled. Ian returned her grin and put an arm around her waist.

"I'm so glad everything is working out between you." The babysitter had her coat on now and was going down the hall towards the front door. "From what Marcus said before he went to bed, I gather he's over the moon about it. He couldn't stop talking about his brilliant Dad, who loves Doctor Who and Buster as much as he does."

Ian glowed with pleasure. Josephine opened the front door for her friend.

"Now, remember if you ever need anyone to sit for your girls, give me a shout!"

"I've got to talk Peter into taking me out first. You've got a diamond there, Josephine. Don't let him go this time!"

"You've got a very perceptive friend." Ian said as the door closed. His voice was slow and teasing.

Gently he pulled her towards him and bent to kiss her. Her response was hesitant and lacked the immediate electricity he'd shared with Sandra.

"Do you mind being kissed by me?" he asked her.

"Whenever we get close I imagine you paying someone."

"I didn't kiss her."

"No, I hear they don't do kissing."

"Perhaps if we …" He indicated upstairs.

"I'm not sure I'm ready."

"I thought we were nicely relaxed after a pleasant evening together. Marcus is fast asleep and it's only 11 p.m. The night is still young." He reached for her mouth again.

"No." She pulled away. "We've been divorced for nearly five years and back together only a week. These things take time. I can't just jump into bed with you."

Later, Ian lay in the spare room single bed, waiting for it to warm up with his body heat. As sleep drew close, his mind wandered to Sandra. He had a very pleasant dream.

***

Sandra knelt down to be on a level with her daughter.

"Chelsea's mummy has been very kind. She says you can sleep at their house every Thursday while I go to night school."

"Why do you need to go to school?"

"I want to get better at Maths and English so that I

204

can pass exams and get a more interesting job. I'm going to learn about computers as well, but that's during the day."

"You can already read and write and add up the ironing money."

"I need a certificate to prove I can do those things. It will be something to show I'm clever and it will get me a better job."

"I think you're clever already!"

Halifax flung her arms around her mother's neck and gave her a kiss.

"Do you mind going to Chelsea's? The English class is tonight."

"I don't mind. Chelsea is my very bestest friend and I love her the most after I love you."

Sandra ruffled her daughter's hair. She was lucky to have such a lovely little girl, who seemed unharmed by her single-parent upbringing in basic surroundings.

It was a bus ride to the college where the GCSE English Language class was being held. It was a shame she'd already missed half a term of lessons but Sandra couldn't wait until the following September to start her quest for self-improvement. The short time she'd spent with Ian had shown her that his sort of people were really only the same as her, except that they'd made the most of a proper education. Education meant a good job that paid more than the supermarket café or taking in ironing. Sandra was determined to get herself that job and build an easier life for Halifax. Her daughter would be properly educated from the start. There was no reason why she and Halifax shouldn't have as bright a future as Ian and Marcus. It might take them a bit longer but they'd get there in the end.

The classroom was already full of chattering men and women taking off coats, getting out books and checking they had a pen that worked. For a moment Sandra stood on the threshold dumbstruck. They all knew each other. They all looked clever. They'd all been here six weeks already. A few of them wore Doc Martens and leggings like her, but none had wisps of odd-coloured hair escaping from a scarf.

"Can I help you?" asked a woman standing at the front.

As she spoke, the eyes of everyone else in the room swivelled towards the door. Sandra wanted to turn and run. Why on earth did she ever think she could fit in at a college? She wasn't as clever as these people. She should have learned her lesson from the way Ian had rejected her as second best.

"When I came to enrol the woman said it would be all right to start the course late. They said you could let me know what I'd missed."

The woman referred to some papers in front of her.

"Ah yes. Sandra, isn't it? Take a seat please. I'll talk to you at the end of the lesson about catching up."

Sandra headed towards the back of the room and then realised those seats were at a premium and had all been taken. Reluctantly she sat on the second row and hoped the teacher and her fellow students would take no notice of her.

The evening class surprised her. It wasn't like being at school. The teacher was interesting and Sandra was able to follow the lesson without much difficulty. It was like stepping into another world, away from greasy café tables, bags of creased clothes and the dingy surroundings of Vesey Villa.

Where Sandra had grown up, people didn't read books. But now she began to learn that reading books was both a way of escaping reality and a way of learning.

Ian Wolvestone had done Sandra a favour. He may have dumped her but he'd also shown her there was a better way of living. And she was going to grab hold of it.

***

Ignatius reached Vesey Villa just before eight in the morning. He positioned himself to the side of the house, just in front of the gate that led to the back garden. He was out of obvious sight but could see who came and went. It shouldn't be long before Miss Purple Hair and her daughter emerged to walk to school.

He watched a district nurse arrive in a Mini. She parked and let herself into the building carrying a business-like black holdall. A wave of relief washed over him: Betty hadn't died in his absence. Maybe in a few days' time, when the coast was clear, he'd drop some shopping anonymously on her doorstep. But right now he needed to concentrate.

A few minutes later his prey came out on to the paved driveway.

"Zip your coat up, Halifax. It's cold today. I don't know what happened to the autumn. It feels like winter's here already."

The little girl hopped from one foot to another as her mother fiddled with the jacket and then they set off walking. Ignatius followed at a discreet distance, ready to disappear behind a parked car or garden hedge should either of them turn round.

The plan had come to him during the long hours he'd spent lying on the bed staring at the ceiling in Milton Keynes. He'd been thinking about his lost son. In his mind, Ignatius had named him Tom. If Tom had lived he'd have become Ignatius's most precious possession. Ignatius would have moulded him into the thing he'd never been - a fine, upstanding young man. In return, Tom would have loved his father and cared for him long into the future. Loneliness would have become a thing of the past for Ignatius.

Now he needed a Tom substitute. It was too much to hope he could woo another Maxine. She'd been the only woman ever to take an interest in him. And even if he managed to impregnate another female, she might leave with the child or, like Maxine, turn murderer.

Ignatius needed a child that was his alone. The only child he knew belonged to his purple-haired neighbour. Unfortunately she was a girl. He didn't understand females but maybe this one was young enough to be moulded into a masculine way of thinking. He'd have to take her abroad where she wouldn't be spotted, but she'd be young enough to learn the language and become successful with his guidance. And they'd each have the other to care for them.

Ignatius matched his pace along the pavement to that of the mother and daughter. He was just close enough to hear snatches of their conversation.

"I wish Marcus still lived by us. I don't know why his daddy wouldn't be your boyfriend."

"Marcus and his daddy and his mummy are all living together again now. That's how families should be."

Ignatius had had a mummy and daddy once, but he'd never felt his family was how all families should be. Very soon he'd make sure that Halifax had the daddy she longed for and then she wouldn't need a mummy at all.

The little girl was skipping now and he had to increase his pace to keep up with them. There were more people on the pavement, too, mostly parents with children. The school must be close.

"Chelsea!" the little girl exclaimed, and loosed her mother's grip.

Now the two little girls were holding hands and the two mothers were chatting behind them.

"I'll watch them until the doors open," said the woman Ignatius took to be Chelsea's mum. "You get off to work."

"Thanks. I seem to be rushing around like a headless chicken trying to fit in the college courses as well as everything else."

Parents and children were milling about the tarmac playground now. Ignatius didn't dare follow them through the gates in case anyone noticed him. He didn't know how widely his picture might have been circulated. He'd ditched the woolly hat and scarf, deciding they attracted too much attention. Instead, he'd shaved his head and grown the beginnings of a beard. The reading glasses had stayed and he was losing weight owing to his lack of cash for food. In Milton Keynes he'd lived on a full English breakfast plus six biscuits a day. Mildred (the Comfort Stay landlady had insisted on first name terms) had drawn the line when after eating four slices of toast he'd asked for even more.

"I'll have to charge you extra for that, William," she'd said. Ignatius had immediately cancelled his request.

He'd managed to withdraw a further £200 the day after he arrived in Milton Keynes. But when he tried again the machine ate the card. After that he'd hardly left the guesthouse, afraid the police were combing the town for him. It was lucky he'd had the wit to put a false name on Mildred's registration form.

When the children went into the classroom, Ignatius left the school and walked around the neighbourhood. His plan was only half-formed.

"Impulsive! Impulsive!" he could hear his mother hissing critically in his head.

He knew where he'd take the girl initially, but to smuggle her out of the country he'd need a functioning car with a large boot. Yet even with only half a plan there were preparations to make and things to be procured. With the last of Maxine's cash he went into a DIY superstore, the one he'd used weeks earlier to buy the spade that had buried Maxine. They sold rope and, surprisingly, tea towels. A knife would be useful too. He'd stupidly dropped the other one on the river bank. The female cashier stuffed his purchases into a carrier bag, hardly glancing at Ignatius even when she asked if he had a loyalty card.

In one of the streets behind the school there were road works. Five or six men in fluorescent jackets were doing something with a hole in the tarmac. Temporary traffic lights had been set up. It was lunchtime and the team seemed to be knocking off for a break. A couple of them lit cigarettes and wandered down the street. The others were producing plastic boxes and flasks. Two climbed into their van to eat with the radio going full blast. Another hung his yellow vest on one of the temporary road signs, stretched, and then set off at a brisk walk towards some shops further down the road.

Ignatius sauntered by, trying to ignore the huge sandwiches being eaten by the van men. He peered into the hole at naked pipes. No one took any notice of him. He watched the drivers at the traffic lights drumming their fingers impatiently until red changed through orange to green. They stared straight ahead, oblivious to him.

He walked past the hi-vis vest hung on the sign and paused. Still no one was watching. Everyone was locked in their own private worlds. The vest felt heavier than he expected when he picked it up. He walked quickly behind the van so he couldn't be seen by its occupants and then pulled it on nonchalantly, as though he were just another labourer getting ready for an afternoon's work.

The children were still outside on their lunch break. He could hear them screaming and shouting. He walked close by the railings, being careful not to linger in case one of the supervisors thought he was acting strangely. The little girl, Halifax he'd heard her mother call her, was with three others sitting on a patch of grass near the fence. Perhaps he could take her now. Ignatius leaned on the fence near the girls. He knew what he was going to say.

Then a shrill whistle blew and all the children fled towards the school buildings like ants to a nest. They lined up and then filed into the school. Ignatius moved quickly on.

He would stay close by and catch them at afternoon break. He took off the fluorescent vest and rolled it under his arm. There was a mini-supermarket in the parade of shops. Inside he tried to guess what sort of sweets little girls would prefer. A colourful bag of Starburst might do the trick. He paid extra to get a carrier bag in which to hide the vest until it was time to put it on again.

Ignatius ate two of the Starburst himself whilst sitting on a bench waiting to hear the roar of children being released again. When he heard the youngsters' shouts he pulled on the vest and shoved the screwed-up carrier bag into his pocket. Now he looked official. He palmed a handful of the sweets.

The four girls were standing on the same patch of grass.

"Halifax!" Ignatius called as quietly as he could, so

that she could hear him but the patrolling teacher couldn't. "Halifax!"

He saw one of the other girls nudge her and she turned round.

"Your mum sent me."

She frowned and looked confused.

"She sent a sweet each for you and your friends so you'd know you can trust me."

All four girls came close enough to take the sweets. Ignatius glanced towards the teacher but she was engrossed in sorting out an argument between two boys about a football.

"Mum knows that Starbursts are my favourite," said Halifax.

"That's why she gave them to me to bring to you. You better give me the wrappers. We don't want to get into trouble with your teacher for dropping litter."

He gave the girls half a minute to start chewing the sweets and accept him a bit more.

"Halifax, your mum sent me because she's not feeling well and needs you to come home right away. She says having you back in the flat at Vesey Villa will make her feel better."

"Why did she send you? We don't know you."

"I was working on the road outside Vesey Villa when she arrived home. She fainted on the doorstep. I helped her up to your flat. Number two, isn't it? Then she asked if I could fetch you and gave me these sweets so you'd know it was safe to come with me."

It was a stroke of luck that he'd chosen Halifax's favourite sweets.

"Shall I tell the teacher?"

"No, there's no need to make a fuss. There's not much of the day left and no more registers to mark. Come on, I'll lift you over the fence and then we'll get

212

home quickly to your mum. With you home, she'll be better in no time."

After a slight hesitation Halifax went close to the fence and raised her arms. Ignatius lifted her over and then took her hand.

"Let's see how quickly we can walk without actually running," he said. "Running all the way home will make us puffed out, so a fast walk will get us there much quicker."

As they turned out of sight of the school, the whistle blew to indicate the end of the afternoon break.

Chapter Eighteen

Sandra was deep into her English homework. Once she sat down and really concentrated, it wasn't as hard as she'd expected. The tutor had given them a newspaper article to analyse as part of the non-fiction syllabus. They had to summarise the argument put forward and talk about who the text was aimed at. Sandra was enjoying herself and wondering whether she might make a journalist one day. She often thought about the reporter she'd met on her visit to the college. He hadn't talked in Ian's posh accent; he'd talked like the people around here. So maybe it was possible for her to make something of herself, in the same way that he had done. His business card was now a bookmark in her English textbook and she'd started thinking of it as a good luck charm. According to the card, the reporter's name was David Jones. And now she understood why David was good at his job; he'd been natural and easy to talk to. With him she'd felt like she was talking to a friend not a stranger. She imagined he'd be brilliant at interviewing people.

"Oh my God!"

The radio DJ had just given the time as 3:30pm.

"I'm so sorry, Halifax! I'm on my way!"

Sandra stuffed her feet into shoes, grabbed her bag and keys and shot down the stairs of Vesey Villa.

She half-ran, half-walked to the school and her breath was coming in gasps by the time she got there. It was the first time she'd ever been late to collect her daughter and she was terrified the little girl might be in tears and the teacher about to report her to social services for neglect.

The playground was deserted but noise and laughter came from the open window of the room used by the after school club. Perhaps they'd put Halifax in there and Sandra would be expected to pay for their time.

She went to Halifax's classroom. Mrs Wilkinson, the teacher, was putting up a display of paintings.

"I'm sorry I'm so late," Sandra panted. "I completely forgot the time. Was Halifax upset? I hope you didn't have to stay behind especially to mind her."

"What?" Mrs Wilkinson turned around.

"I've never been late to collect her before." Sandra glanced around the room. "Where is she?"

"Gone. They've all gone home."

"She can't be gone. I wasn't here to collect her."

"But I watch to make sure there's an adult for every child."

"I wasn't here." Sandra couldn't focus on the teacher. Her eyes were roaming the desks, displays and little cupboards on wheels. In a second Halifax would pop up from somewhere like a jack-in-a-box and make them all jump. "She didn't go home with me."

"Are you sure?"

"Of course I'm bloody well sure!"

"We have to tell the head." Mrs Wilkinson put down the painting and staple gun.

The headmistress immediately called the police and instigated a full search of the school buildings and grounds. The caretaker, cleaners and all the teachers dropped what they were doing and checked everywhere. Sandra's mind whirled.

"I wasn't here," she said to the school secretary, who guided her into the office and sat her down with a cup of sweet tea. "I wasn't here. I wasn't here."

"No one's blaming you, love. Besides, she'll turn up any minute now. I'm going to telephone everyone in her class and check she didn't get invited back to a mate's house. Can you tell me who her closest friends are?"

"Chelsea. She sleeps over there sometimes. But it's always pre-arranged."

The police arrived. They asked lots of detailed questions and looked at the register.

Mrs Wilkinson was close to tears, trying to remember if Halifax was in class right up to the end of the day or whether she could have gone missing before the end of afternoon school.

"I don't know. She was definitely here before the afternoon break because I was listening to her reading. Afterwards I'd no specific contact with her. She's always well behaved so she doesn't stand out like the disruptive ones."

At these small words of praise, Sandra began to cry. The school secretary was ready with a box of tissues.

"I'm halfway through phoning around the class," she said, "but so far no one knows anything."

The police took Sandra home and waited whilst she found a recent photo of Halifax in her school uniform. The male officer left with the picture.

"I'd like to stay and ask you some questions," the woman said. "I'm Sergeant Glenning."

Sandra nodded and used a crumpled tissue from her pocket to blow her nose. "Do you want tea? Or coffee?"

"Tea, no sugar. Point me in the right direction and I'll make it."

"No, I'll do it." Sandra gathered up the English homework books from the table. "But I'm right out of biscuits."

"Just as well." Sergeant Glenning patted her stomach. "We get offered too much food in this job."

The two women sat at the table with mugs of tea. Sandra stared at the brown liquid and wondered if the lump in her throat would allow her to drink it. The policewoman pulled out a notebook and started asking questions about Halifax, their usual routines, and whether anyone might have reason to snatch the little girl.

"Her father, perhaps?" the officer prompted.

"No way. We've had absolutely no contact since she was tiny."

"Has anything unusual happened to either of you recently? Have you noticed anyone around the school or this house?"

"No." Sandra blew her nose again and tried to think. "Only that business in the flat next door."

She started to explain about Maxine's disappearance and Ian being coerced into moving the body.

"I'm aware of that." Sergeant Glenning scribbled in her notebook. "Ignatius Smith is still at large. Is there any reason why he might want to hurt Halifax?"

"Do you think it's him? Oh my God! He's a psycho! She could be dead! My baby could be dead!"

Sandra hammered the table with her fists and then raised her head and wailed. There was an acute physical pain in her core, as though someone was trying to tear her life out from within her.

"I can't bear it!"

The policewoman reached over and stroked Sandra's arm.

"At this point we've nothing to suggest that any harm has come to Halifax. Smith is only one line of enquiry and we don't know he's involved. Take a few deep breaths, Sandra. You'll be more help to Halifax if you can stay calm. Is there anybody I can call who can come and be with you? A relative or a friend perhaps?"

Sandra tried to think. Her own family had been worse than useless when she fell pregnant with Halifax; they were hardly likely to come rallying round now. She could call Donna but she'd have to find a babysitter for her own child. Besides, it wasn't Donna that Sandra really wanted at her side right now.

She could think of only one person who'd really understand the hell she was in: Ian. He was devoted to his son and would do anything to protect him. He'd know how she felt. But he was off limits.

"There's no one," Sandra said.

**

Getting the girl had been easier than Ignatius had expected. She'd walked willingly away from the school with him and they'd soon been out of sight of the school buildings. But since they'd halted at a bus shelter, things had got harder.

"Why are we going on the bus?" she'd demanded. "It's quicker to walk."

"We have to go on the bus to the hospital."

"You said Mummy was poorly at home!"

The little girl's voice got louder and people started to stare. He crouched down to her level and spoke softly.

"I didn't want to scare you at school by saying that your Mummy was in the hospital. But the ambulance

218

had to take her there. So that's where we've got to go. She'll tell you what she needs from the flat and give you the key. Then we can go and collect her night things. You're going to be a great help to your mummy. She told me what a good girl you are and said to make sure you had your favourite sweets. What colour Starburst would you like next?"

"Orange."

The girl's voice was subdued and her expression was doubtful. Ignatius took off the luminous vest; he'd no need to draw attention to himself as a labourer now. On the bus he ushered her into a window seat and sat next to her. Fewer people would notice them if she had her head turned to the window and it would be more difficult for her to make a dash for freedom. He placed the carrier bag between his feet. Halifax said nothing on the bus ride.

As the bus approached the multi-storey car park, Ignatius took her hand and they got off.

"Is this the hospital? It doesn't look like Holby City."

"We have to walk through the car park to get there. Hold my hand. We'll go all the way to the top and then you can see the hospital. We might even see Mummy waving at us."

Ignatius felt the small soft hand slip into his as they entered the dismal concrete structure. Her trust infused him with a strange warm feeling.

More cars than usual were parked on the lower floors, commuters not yet finished at the office. But few people were to be seen, and those who did appear were more interested in reaching their cars and escaping home than in a bald man with glasses chaperoning a small girl.

On the top deck there wasn't a single car. The light was beginning to fade and it was exposed and windy.

"I don't like it here. I want Mummy."

Halifax's voice was clogged with unshed tears. Ignatius sensed that trouble wasn't far away.

"I know somewhere cosy where we can sit and wait until Mummy's ready for us," he said.

The concrete kiosk was empty, as he knew it would be.

"Sit down." He gently pushed Halifax against the bench.

"No. It's horrible in here. This isn't a waiting room. I want Mummy!"

"You must sit here quietly or Mummy won't come."

Ignatius couldn't stop his voice becoming sharp. Why didn't she just obey him as he'd obeyed his parents?

"Where is she?" Halifax's words turned into an anguished yowl.

Ignatius slammed his hand over her mouth.

"Be quiet!"

There was a sharp pain in his right leg as she lifted a small foot and kicked him.

"Bitch!"

She kicked him on the other leg.

He removed his hand from her mouth and slapped her hard across the face. She let out a yelp. He slapped her again. She sat down on the bench, tears in her eyes, but not sobbing. Scarlet hand-prints marked her face.

"Lie down!"

Halifax did as she was told.

The new serrated vegetable knife was lying on top of everything else in the carrier bag. He placed it on the floor and then pulled out the length of rope. When he'd bought these things he'd hoped not to have to use them. And when he'd felt Halifax's small trusting hand in his, all had seemed well. But now she was playing up it was satisfying to see her terror as she looked at the blade. He would teach her to obey him.

He uncoiled an arm's length of the rope and then picked up the knife and cut it with one sharp movement. He wound it around her ankles, pulled it tight until she winced and then fastened it off.

"No!" she shouted.

He slapped her again.

"Why don't you learn? I don't like noise! Be quiet!"

Ignatius tied her wrists behind her back in the same way he'd trussed her legs. Then he sat her up so her wriggling wouldn't make her fall from the bench and smash her head on the hard concrete. The last thing he wanted was another dead body on his hands. But she started wailing and making a real hullabaloo. She jerked her limbs backwards and forwards as if trying to loosen the bonds.

"Shut up!" Ignatius yelled.

He pulled the tea towel from the carrier bag. He fashioned it into a gag, forced it between her teeth and tied it in a double knot at the back of her head. He felt her wince as her hair was caught in the twisted cloth. Halifax's hysterical screams became muffled grunts and Ignatius started to assemble his thoughts in a coherent order. He needed to steal a car, drive it to a port and board a ferry with the girl hidden. A car with sat-nav was imperative because Ignatius had no idea how to get to Dover, which was the only port he knew.

"Now you're starting to think ahead. That's good," his mother whispered.

Ignatius felt a tiny glow of pride.

***

Ian was setting the table for dinner when the phone in

221

his pocket rang. Josephine was hovering at his shoulder with a wooden salad bowl and matching servers, waiting for him to put out the place mats.

"Don't answer it," she said. "The lasagne's almost done and I need you to pour the fruit juice and call Marcus downstairs."

Ian glanced at the screen but didn't take the call. He was surprised to see it was Sandra. There'd been no communication between them since that day in the hotel. She'd left a voice message. He'd listen to it later when he was alone.

"Dinner's ready!" Josephine brought the plates into the dining room.

Ian's phone beeped and he automatically touched the screen to read the text. It was Sandra again and she'd sent a single word, 'Urgent'. He shoved the phone back in his pocket and picked up his knife and fork.

"You are coming on Saturday, aren't you Dad? No, I don't want that much salad, Mum."

"The best football players have a healthy diet, Marcus."

Josephine put more green leaves on her son's plate.

"Dad? The match on Saturday morning?"

"What did you say?"

Ian could hear his ex-wife and son speaking across the table but his mind was on the urgent message from Sandra. She wouldn't cry wolf.

"It's my first match as captain. You'll be there?"

"Of course he'll be there, won't you, Ian?"

"My son's first match as captain - I wouldn't miss it for the world!"

Sandra wouldn't contact him unless it was important. The lasagne was sticking around his mouth. He couldn't carry on eating without knowing what was wrong.

"Excuse me. I have to check my voicemail."

Ian wiped his lips and put his napkin down.

"Not in the middle of a meal! Surely it can wait?"

"It's urgent."

Ian walked out of the room. He went into the utility and closed the door behind him.

"Ian, it's Sandra."

Her voice was choked with sobs.

"You've got to come. Ignatius Smith has taken Halifax. I don't know who else to turn to. Please come!"

There were more words but they became incoherent. Ian leaned against the tiled wall and tried to process what he'd just heard. Buster jumped up to get his attention.

"Later, boy. Later."

He could picture Sandra alone in the bedsit, distraught with fear for her daughter. He had to be with her.

"I'm sorry. I've got to go out." He poked his head into the dining room. "A friend's in trouble."

Josephine looked alarmed. "Surely you can finish your meal first. There are blueberries for dessert - with ice cream instead of yoghurt if you prefer."

"Ice cream!" Marcus's eyes lit up. "You've got to stay, Dad."

"It's urgent."

Ian patted his pockets to check for wallet and car keys. Josephine followed him out to the hall and spoke quietly.

"Please don't go, Ian. When you're secretive like this I lose faith in you again. What's so urgent that you can't explain it to me?"

She looked close to tears. Telling her about his friendship with Sandra and his urge to help would only upset her more.

"I'm not visiting a prostitute. Like I said, a friend's in trouble."

"If you can't stay for me then stay for Marcus's sake."

Ian sighed. Marcus was his weak point and Josephine knew it. But Sandra's anguished voicemail played in his head. He remembered spirited little Halifax in the playground.

"I'll explain to him why I have to go."

Ian sat down next to his son. Josephine hovered.

"You remember Sandra and Halifax from Vesey Villa?"

Marcus nodded. "Halifax is cool."

"Well, they need a bit of help tonight and probably tomorrow as well. There's no time to explain it all now, but I have to go to help a friend."

"I understand, Dad."

"That's a good lad. Now, give Buster a long walk for me tonight!"

"I understand, too," Josephine hissed at the front door. "For some reason that woman is more important than me." She held her hand out. "Car keys, please. I need my car in the morning. Take a taxi to your fancy woman."

The police still had Ian's car and he didn't want it back, ever. He could never drive it again after it had transported a dead body. It would have to be sold. He called a taxi and listened again to Sandra's voicemail as he waited at the end of the drive.

***

Now that night was coming it was getting cold in the concrete kiosk. Ignatius planned to choose his car the following morning when all the commuters had parked and disappeared to their offices. The girl was whimpering unintelligibly under the gag. From the increasing smell, Ignatius guessed she'd wet herself or worse. He too wanted to relieve himself. Unable to bear the burning in his bladder any longer, he stood in one of the concrete corners with his back to the girl and unzipped his trousers. After that, the stench in the small room got worse.

He was hungry too. He wished he'd brought food and drink. It was going to be a long night. Because of her smell he was no longer sitting on the bench next to Halifax. Instead, he crouched against the wall just inside the doorway. Every so often he stuck his head out and breathed in a lungful of clean air.

The minutes crawled by. Ignatius tried to entertain himself with thoughts of the future and how quickly the girl would come to love and respect him. He would mould her life into the best it could be. Her head was drooping to one side now. She was falling asleep. It was much pleasanter when her muffled sobbing stopped. Being careful not to breathe near her, he moved her from a sitting to a lying position on the bench so she could sleep more easily and leave him in peace.

His stomach was angry at the lack of food. His head ached with dehydration. In this state Ignatius couldn't think through the details of his plan. If he didn't get it right he'd be going to prison instead of across the Channel. He'd have to take a small risk to avoid a bigger risk tomorrow. He needed food. There was a burger place opposite the multi-storey car park. He wouldn't be gone much more than five minutes, ten at the most. The girl was sleeping and she wouldn't get far bound and gagged. He'd wait until the evening rush had died down and then he'd get something to eat.

***

"Ian, you came!"

"You haven't got the chain on the door."

"Fuck the chain. There's no time for that. I have to get Halifax back."

Until that moment, Sandra hadn't been sure he'd come. She'd thought his ex-wife might be more important. He had no obligation to her or Halifax. They stood and looked at each other. Then he pulled her close and hugged her as if he'd never let go. It felt good, it felt right. For a split second, Sandra forgot her daughter was missing. Then the misery and panic were back. She pulled away from him.

"What am I going to do? How will I get her back?"

"Where are the police? What are they doing?"

"Searching, circulating Halifax's picture - all the things you see on TV, I guess. A policewoman will be back here soon."

"They're treating Ignatius as the prime suspect?"

"Yes. I don't know. They're not as sure as I am."

The last words were almost drowned by Sandra's sobs.

Ian led her to the settee and she told him the whole story from the time she'd arrived late at the school.

"OK. Let's think this through logically. Perhaps we can deduce where he's taken her."

For the first time since she'd realised that Halifax was missing, Sandra's brain started to function coherently. Ian was a calming influence. He'd know how to get her daughter back.

"Places we know are associated with Ignatius Smith." He held up a hand to check them off on his fingers. "Here - Vesey Villa; the Golden Swan where his car was parked; Derby from where he posted the cards; the riverbank where I … we … Maxine's body went in; and the multi-storey car park where his mother … died."

"Wouldn't he go somewhere we'd never suspect?"

"Possibly. But if he did, where would we start looking? The police have probably checked the obvious places but he may be moving her around. He could come back to the places they've already searched."

"The police aren't sure Ignatius has got her." Sandra blew her nose. She didn't want to think about Halifax being bundled from pillar to post, tired, cold, hungry and very, very frightened. "We have to do something ourselves."

Ian put his arm around her.

"I'll start in the back garden here. That shed would make some sort of hideout. Then I'll cross the road to the Golden Swan. Have you got a torch?"

Sandra searched the cupboard under the sink.

"Here's one that Halifax takes to Brownie sleepovers. It's only small."

When Ian had gone down the stairs, Sandra turned the big light off so she could watch his torch moving around the garden. He disappeared into the shed for a few moments and then re-appeared. He paid special attention to the place where Maxine had been buried. Sandra's fingers were tightly crossed. If he found Halifax in the garden, she'd probably be … Sandra clenched her fists to stop her mind careering down that route.

Eventually Ian disappeared down the side path. Sandra went and stood in Halifax's partitioned bedroom. Very faintly, she could detect her daughter's sleepy smell. She picked up Tigger and held him close as she watched Ian cross the road to the pub. The dot of torchlight proceeded slowly around the perimeter of the car park. Then it went around the pub and out of sight.

Sandra buried her face in Tigger's plushness. This silky softness against her skin was what Halifax experienced when she snuggled down to sleep each night. Except tonight.

The torchlight re-appeared and was then snapped off. Sandra could see Ian's profile under a streetlamp as he waited to re-cross the road. He reached the paved frontage of Vesey Villa at the same time as a police car. He waited whilst the female officer got out. Then he appeared to be telling her something. Sandra rushed downstairs to let them in. The woman might have some news.

"I've got to nip off now," he said as soon as she opened the door. "I'll come back later and stay the night."

"Oh."

What more could she say with the policewoman there?

"I still don't have a car." He pointed to his phone. "Got to call a taxi."

"I wish you'd told me about your boyfriend earlier," the policewoman said when they were back in the bedsit, "especially since he's the one who helped move that body."

"He's not …"

"What's his relationship with Halifax like? Do they get on?" the officer interrupted.

"They get on fine but he's not my boyfriend."

"I've asked him to report to the station in the morning and give a statement. It's routine to talk to people who've had any sort of a relationship with a missing child. Now, can you tell me more about Halifax's father?

Chapter Nineteen

The taxi dropped Ian outside Brilliant Burgers, opposite the multi-storey car park. He decided to search from the top down and took the stairs instead of going the long way up the vehicle ramps. After the first flight he could hear noises ahead. There was someone else in the stairwell. He stopped and listened. The other footsteps were slow.

It was probably someone returning to his car but Ian wanted to be sure before he made himself visible. At the bottom of the next flight he peered upwards around the concrete banister. Ignatius Smith was just disappearing around the next turn in the stairs. He was eating a burger.

Ian froze. Then his body reacted. His knees went weak, he trembled and his stomach churned. He seemed to feel the serrated knife at his neck again. He didn't want to get any closer to the monster. He'd come here only to appease Sandra. He hadn't expected to find anything.

He made his feet walk up the next set of stairs. His shoes were like lead. He wasn't a hero; apprehending criminals wasn't something he could attempt. It was time to call the police.

No signal.

Inside this concrete monstrosity there was no mobile phone signal. There might be a few bars' worth when he got to the top, or he could run back down to Brilliant Burgers and call the police from there.

"What the fuck?" Ignatius' words carried clearly. "Where are you? Where, the fuck, are you?"

No time to call the cops. Something had happened to throw Ignatius off balance. Assuming the monster had Halifax, what would he do if things were going wrong? What might he do if he discovered Ian following him? A brief vision of Marcus without a father passed through his mind. But things had gone too far. He couldn't chicken out now.

Ian reached the top of the stairs. Ignatius was stood in the doorway of a concrete kiosk. The type of weak electric light that lit the stairwell lit the kiosk as well. The rest of the car park was in darkness. As far as Ian could make out they were the only people on the top level. There were no vehicles and nowhere for a small girl to hide. The only way of escape was down the ramps. Ignatius must have had the same thought; he was heading for the nearest slope. Ian followed. He switched on Halifax's torch and kept it pointed away from Ignatius.

A thud made them both stop. Ian moved behind a concrete pillar. Ignatius stood at the top of the ramp and slowly turned 360 degrees. Ian followed the murderer's gaze. There was a large rectangular wheeled rubbish container near to the wall opposite the ramp.

Ignatius went towards it. Ian followed him. If Halifax was to be found, Ian didn't want him getting to her on his own. They reached the container at the same time. Ian shone the torch behind it and Ignatius spotted him. At the same time, they both saw Halifax lying between the wall and the container.

The torch picked out the terror in her eyes. She grunted and sobbed into a gag. Her hands and feet were tied. Ian wanted to lunge for the little girl. But that would make them both easy prey for Ignatius and whatever weapon he might have. Instead, he shone the torch towards the murderer. The light reflected off a metal blade. Ian trembled. This time his assailant might not be lenient with the knife.

Gambling on the element of surprise, Ian threw himself at the other man's legs and rugby-tackled him to the floor. A second later his right shoulder throbbed with intense pain. But he had an advantage. Ignatius was winded and underneath him, and the knife had vanished. Ian dragged himself up to sit on his opponent's stomach. He stamped his feet as hard as he could on Ignatius' hands. Then he whacked the torch at his victim's head with his left hand. The body beneath him struggled less and less.

Ian didn't dare stand up. His opponent wasn't even unconscious, only temporarily stunned. Halifax was out of sight. He didn't know if she was hurt. The pain in his shoulder was getting worse. When Ignatius pulled himself together, Ian wouldn't have the strength to fight back.

There was a thud. Followed by another. And then another.

Ian pointed the torch at the rubbish container. Halifax was emerging by rocking herself backwards and forwards. Free of the container, she rolled slowly and clumsily over to Ian.

The child was a mess. Her hair was matted and her face was grazed. Her school uniform was grey with dust and dirt from the concrete floor. And she smelled foul.

Placing the torch on the floor he undid the gag.

Halifax gasped like someone dragged to shore after almost drowning. She sucked in the air greedily and looked as though she was about to speak.

Ignatius turned his head and his eyes flicked up and down over Halifax. Ian felt the man's body move beneath him. He hit him with the torch again, leaving a red mark on his assailant's temple. Ignatius lay still with his eyes shut.

In the weak torchlight, Ian caught Halifax's eye and placed a finger over his lips to indicate she should say nothing. The sound of her voice might trigger another reaction in Ignatius. He struggled to untie the rope on her ankles. The knot was tight and his right arm had become clumsy. Her white socks were filthy and her black school shoes scuffed from their part in propelling her along the car park floor. But now the rope was off her legs. There was no time to undo her wrists. He indicated that she should run for help.

Halifax wobbled to her feet like a new born foal testing out its skinny legs. Ian gestured with his good arm, urging her to go quickly. She disappeared from their tiny circle of light into the blackness.

With Halifax safely gone, Ian's adrenaline started to diminish. Each time Ignatius moved, Ian hit him with the torch and stamped on his hands, but each time the blows were getting weaker. The pain in his right shoulder was taking over his senses. Slowly, he comprehended: Ignatius' knife was stuck in his shoulder and the damp feeling on his back was blood.

His eyelids hovered on the brink of closure. It was a battle to stay upright. Ignatius moved. Ian flailed ineffectually towards his head with the torch. Ignatius attempted to drag his hands from beneath Ian's feet and raise his upper body from the floor. With a reflex action, Ian bore down on his assailant's palms with his heels. Ignatius yelped with pain.

The status quo remained for some minutes. The battery in the torch failed. Ian felt odd. Between his legs, Ignatius was still. Too still. The blackness came and went with the movement of the clouds across the moon. A distant police siren wailed. Then, like a monster in a film, Ignatius rose in one great movement. Ian toppled off him.

"Marcus, I love you," he whispered, cowering on his side awaiting the final blow. "Grow up to be a good man. And always carry a part of me with you. A part of you will always be with me."

Ignatius towered above him. Ian looked at the feet alongside his head. Soon it would all be over. Soon the blackness would be absolute and forever. He closed his eyes. He didn't want to see the fatal blow coming. Instead, he visualised his son and braced himself to take whatever was about to come his way.

**

The policewoman was asking question after question. It was just like on TV when they tried to twist things around and make the victim into the perpetrator. Finally, Sandra snapped.

"Stop it! Stop trying to turn me into a neglectful mother! Stop trying to give me a love life full of men who at the slightest chance will grab my daughter and harm her! For the last time, there are no men in my life! It's been over a year since I've been out with anyone!"

The policewoman gazed at her and said nothing.

"Why aren't you out looking for Ignatius Smith? He's the one who's got her!"

"As I explained, Sandra, he's part of our investigation but without solid evidence we have to keep an open mind and explore all avenues."

As Sandra flailed in her dark pit of grief, the sergeant's phone rang.

"They've found her." The policewoman was touching Sandra's shoulder gently.

"Is she …?"

The whole world stopped. This was the inevitable terrible moment. Ever since she'd arrived late at the school everything had been building up towards this. She wondered if Ian would come with her to the mortuary.

"Halifax is fine." Sergeant Glenning's face broke into a smile. "Grazed, bruised and in need of a good bath, but other than that she's fine."

Sandra's knees gave way and she sank to the carpet. For a few seconds she sat rocking on the floor as thoughts swirled and settled into yet another new pattern.

"Thank God! Thank God!"

In the space of a few hours, life had gone from normal to hell and now it was heading back towards normal.

"We have to go to the hospital."

The policewoman helped Sandra to her feet.

"I thought you said she was fine."

"She is. It's just a precautionary check-up. Why don't you bring her some favourite clothes? We might need to keep what she's wearing now for forensics and some of it's soiled."

Halifax was in a hospital gown sitting on the bed in a side-room when they arrived. Neither mother nor daughter could speak. Instead they just held each other for a very long time.

Eventually, Halifax said: "Ian saved me."

"Ian saved you?"

Then the whole story came out.

"Halifax raised the alarm at Brilliant Burgers," explained a constable, "and we arrived just as Ignatius was fleeing the top level of the car park. Unfortunately, Ian's been stabbed in the shoulder and kicked a few times. He's in surgery now but he should make a good recovery."

A couple of hours later, Sandra was allowed to see Ian.

"His wife's with him," the nurse said, "but I'm sure she won't mind you popping in."

"Ex-wife," Sandra corrected, surprised at the surge of jealousy she felt.

The nurse was holding the door open to a small private room. Ian lay in the bed. He was too far away for her to tell whether his eyes were open or closed. The woman at his side had her back to the door and she didn't turn round at the sound of visitors. She was clutching Ian's hand and speaking softly to him.

Sandra knew there was no room for her in that tableau. Irrespective of her feelings for Ian, she wasn't a husband stealer. She shook her head at the nurse and walked back down the corridor to where Halifax was being kept overnight for observation.

＊＊＊

Ignatius sat on the narrow bed in the police cell. Maxine was leaning on the closed door and his mother was stood at the opposite end of the cell. Above her head was a tiny barred window. They were shouting across the room at one another.

"He's not normal because of the way you brought him up!" accused Maxine. "You never showed him any love."

"I beg your pardon, young lady. You sent him over the edge when you killed his baby."

"But by then, he'd already pushed you over the edge!"

Maxine screamed with laughter.

Ignatius put his head in his hands. How could two women who'd never even met have such a ding-dong? Thankfully they both shut up when the policeman came back. He started talking about a doctor being on his way and something about a secure unit in a hospital. Behind the officer, Maxine pointed one finger at her head and twirled it - just like the sixth form bullies used to do to him in the common room.

Ignatius lunged towards her, his arms raised. The policeman caught him sharply by the wrists and shouted for reinforcements.

Ignatius's mother rolled her eyes and shook her head.

Epilogue

It rained twelve months later, on the day Ian and Josephine re-married. No one minded because the joy radiating from the bride and groom more than compensated for the lack of sunshine. The pageboy wore a kilt. He walked down the aisle solemn-faced and responsible, leading an overexcited spaniel. When the groom was allowed to kiss the bride, the congregation cheered. The pageboy rolled his eyes heavenward.

All three of them started the evening's dancing to 'We are Family' by Sister Sledge. Much later, when the partying was over and Marcus had finally been persuaded that it was bedtime, Ian and Josephine toasted their future in room service champagne.

"I thought I was going to lose you that night they called me to the hospital." Josephine ran her fingers along her new husband's lips and then down towards his chest. "That's when I knew for certain I still loved you."

Ian placed his mouth on hers. There was no mistaking the strength of the voltage between them.

***

The secure hospital suited Ignatius. He liked the locked doors. He felt safe. There was routine. Every morning his tablets arrived. Then there were therapy sessions or woodwork. He even did creative writing sometimes. Maxine and his mother no longer troubled him. Life seemed on an even keel. And he had Teddy Bear for company.

***

Sandra grinned broadly when she saw which journalist the local paper had sent. David Jones seemed equally pleased. He made Sandra turn this way and that as he tried to get the best shot for his 'Adult Learner of the Year' article. Sandra had achieved straight As in her English, Maths and IT GCSEs.

"I'm impressed at your progress since we first met. What are your plans for the future?"

David's notebook was at the ready. There was that familiar flirtatious twinkle in his eye when he looked up from his shorthand and smiled at her.

"I want to train as a primary school teacher."

"Any particular reason?"

His face reflected the interest Sandra was feeling in him.

"I want a career that will fit around my daughter," she said, to remind him of the full facts of her situation before he said or did anything he might regret.

He appeared to consider this statement before asking his next question.

"Do you find it difficult to get babysitters?"

"I have favours I can call in from friends."

"Good. Would you like to go for a drink tomorrow night?"

OTHER BOOKS PUBLISHED BY WORDPLAY

Losing Hope by Nikki Dee

In 1995 a small girl vanished from her home. No trace of her was found though her family never stopped looking. In 2010 a damaged and vulnerable young woman is rescued from a burning building. Can this possibly be that long lost child and, if so, where has she been and why?

The Cardinals of Schengen by Michael Barton

Jack Hudson, the UK Government's Foreign Secretary, is assassinated in his own home. In attempting to discover his brother's murderer, Peter Hudson finds himself in a race against time to save Europe from a secret society determined to see Europe become the Fourth Reich.

Precinct 25 by Various Authors

25 stories, 25 murders, each taking 25 minutes to read. For those that like their New York killings potted, this is the perfect coffee table crime anthology.

Keep Write On by Ian Govan

Published posthumously, *Keep Write On* is a collection of Ian's musings on life and, in particular, writing. There is wit, tinged with a little life cynicism here and there, that will make you giggle inside. WordPlay: 'encouraging writers to write, and then getting them read'.

42951169R00146

Printed in Poland
by Amazon Fulfillment
Poland Sp. z o.o., Wrocław